GARFIELD

GRIFFIN BROTHERS BOOK 3

KATHI S. BARTON

World Castle Publishing, LLC
Pensacola, Florida
Copyright © Kathi S. Barton 2023
Hardback ISBN: 9798373264938
Paperback ISBN: 9781960076182
eBook ISBN: 9781960076199
First Edition World Castle Publishing, LLC, January 11, 2023
http://www.worldcastlepublishing.com
Licensing Notes
Cover: Karen Fuller
Editor: Karen Fuller

Prologue

Charles, Charlie to most people who knew him, was so lost that he hadn't any idea if he was walking on the ground or the sky. He knew the difference, of course, but it was so dark out tonight that if there had been a moon shining, he couldn't see it. When he sat himself down on a log to get his bearings again, he paused in his thinking to look at what could have made the sound he'd heard.

Terrified out of his mind when he saw glowing eyes looking at him, Charlie sat as still as he could. The eyes grew larger and incredibly more shiny as the beast made his way to him. He didn't run, knowing that even if he knew where he was at the moment, the wolf would know it better. It would chase him down and kill him without any hesitation.

The wolf, a big gray fella, just stood there within a few inches of his outstretched legs. When he laid down, putting his heavy head onto his leg, Charlie had another moment of fear. The thing never took his eyes off him either. As soon as he felt he was brave enough to try and talk to the wolf, he was gone and in his place was a man.

A fully clothed man with the gray of the wolf's fur colored into his hair. Even his eyes were the same as the wolf, Charlie thought. Still, neither of them moved until the man sat back on his butt and regarded him.

"You live on the property not far from here. Is that correct?" Charlie told him he was only squatting there until they found him. But he was a mite lost. "Yes, I've been following you for some time. And in all that time, did you harm any other animal you came across, and there were plenty too. Why is that?"

"You mean the rabbit and the family of deer?" The man nodded. "I don't have a need for meat just now. I only kill when I have to. When my belly feels like it can't go another minute without some meat in it. And even then, I use it up to the best I can. What I can't use, I find some other animal that will use the rest. Why do you ask?"

"I'll get to that. You didn't seem that surprised when I changed from wolf to man. Can you tell me why that is?" He nodded and told him what he'd been seeing a lot of lately. "Yes, war will make a man wish for better times. So you were surprised but just wrote it off as being another strange thing that had no explanation. That's a very good reason, I think."

"They say that the war is about over. I don't know much about that. I can still hear shooting when I'm out and about. I don't have any land left because the soldiers took it all when they was coming through. Not that it was much more than a bunch of rocks and stumps, to begin with." The man only nodded. "I'm Charles Griffin. Most call me Charlie. A great deal more, but I ignore them. Not everybody was able to go to school all the time. I had my family to feed when my daddy up and got sick. Momma died a few weeks ago, and I've been roaming around since looking for work. I don't suppose you know anyone that might be wanting an extra hand around or two, do you?"

"I do, as a matter of fact. My name is Romeo Hank. The Hank is for when I need a last name. But I do have something that I'd like to propose to you if you've got the time to listen." Charlie told him he didn't have anything but time right now. "All right. "I have a medium-sized pack. You can see a few of them over there watching over us. They're all just wolves. I'm the only wolf shifter that I know. They're a good bunch. Hungry most of the time but then all of us are, correct?"

"Yes. Some more than others. At least I can find me a bit of string and fashion me up a hook to use." Romeo told him that was excellent. "You need me to fish some fish out for you and your pack? I don't mind at all doing that for you. In fact, I'd be powerful happy to help you out."

"Not just yet. But I think that I will take you up on it soon. I have a daughter. Her name is Luna. Such a beautiful name, don't you think?" Charlie asked if it meant moon. "It does. Thank you. You're very well educated for a man with no means of living."

"My mom was a school teacher when I was born. They fired her, of course, when she had me. She didn't know my daddy, so that didn't help her none. She taught me to read and to figure. I can write too, but I do have to think about the spelling of things. Can you write?" Romeo said that he'd been given a great gift in that. "I think so too. When I find me a newspaper or some little old book, I treasure it for a bit. Then I pass it on if I can. I don't have to know the people in the paper. I just like reading about their stories. Are you going to tell me what this is about?"

"I am. I was working up to it, but I believe you to be a man that can be trusted with things in life. I would like to change you into a wolf. One such as I am. You'll be a man when you wish. A wolf when necessary. There will be magic as well as wealth." Charlie told him he didn't have use for wealth, but food all the time would be nice. "That is precisely what I'm speaking about, Charlie, my good man."

Throughout the rest of the night and well into the morning, they spoke of things that Romeo needed from him. It wasn't brought up again about him being changed, but Romeo did tell him that his daughter had found out that he, plain old Charlie was her mate. The sole reason that he'd not been harmed while wandering around in the woods.

"Do you understand what it is I want you to do?" Charlie said that he thought so. "No. I'm sorry. I can't allow you to go into this, only thinking you understand. Please, ask me anything that you'd like. You must be clear on this. I need for you to be clear on how it is I wish for you to someday take over for me."

Romeo never got upset with him when he asked his questions. If Charlie was honest with himself, which he usually tried not to be, he was afraid that Romeo had picked the wrong man. That he'd be better off finding himself someone else to take over his empire.

"You're the right man, Charlie. When I told you that I'd been following you around, I wanted you to know that it wasn't just last evening. But for some time now. I've seen you share your last bit of food with people. Work for someone that cannot do for themselves and not take anything but a bit of bread and water. You're a very good man. A better man that I am." Charlie started to protest. "No. I'm correct in picking you as my replacement. And if that is some of your worries, being an Alpha, you've no worries there either. I will not leave this earth for the next until you are comfortable with what is needed of you. Now. If you've no more questions, I shall leave you to allow you to think on it. I'll be back here tomorrow so that you can tell me your answer. I know I have picked the right man, Charlie. It's something that you can do easily to save this pack and my daughter."

Luna followed him as he walked around. He'd thought about calling back Romeo and asking more questions, but he didn't. Sitting down again, his leg bothering him from sitting so long, he looked at the big, beautiful wolf.

"You're not really his daughter, are you?" She shook her head. "I didn't think so. Is there any more of the others that he claims are his children?" She nodded this time, and he determined by asking questions that it was one other female. "I don't know what to think about all this, to be honest with you. Are you my mate? Is he telling me the truth? I just don't know what to think."

She nodded or shook her head after each of the questions he put to her. Yes, she was his mate. Yes, Romeo was telling the truth. There were many more questions and answers. He was headed back to the area where he'd first seen Romeo when he felt the pain take his breath away as it slammed into his left shoulder.

Falling back, he hit his head and lay there while trying his best to catch his breath. That was when he heard the other gunshots, the wolf howling and trying to hide. Pulling Luna toward him, he whispered harshly into her ear, hoping that at least she'd understand him enough to know that she must warn the others.

"Go. Tell Romeo to hide the pack. To make sure you and your sister are safe." She didn't want to leave him, whimpering at him as she laid her head on his shoulder. "Go. Please. Run and escape before they hurt you too."

When she left him, Charlie closed his eyes. Opening them when he felt the shadow darken over him, he looked up in time to see the barrel of a large rifle. He was a goner. He knew that. He could only hope that Luna and the others were safe.

~*~

Thousands of years later....

Boo watched the young woman he'd been watching over since she'd been nothing but a wee babe. He wasn't told anything. Not the way of it, nor how long he'd been set to watch her. In all the twenty-six years since the day she'd been birthed, he'd kept her in his sight and safe from harm as best he could. But today wasn't going to be a good day for her. Or him, for that matter.

The woman was having a good life, he supposed. Good parents. A brother and a sister, both older than her, that weren't aware of her, he thought. Sable had a good-paying job, and she was wealthy. Not that a person would ever know that. Never flaunting her wealth nor what she did for a living, she lived like a pauper. Her parents, too, had a good deal of money, and they were very generous with it. Not that he knew any of them all that well. Just Lady James.

Late last night, he'd been notified that he needed to go to his boss. Lady James had saved his life when she'd been younger than the miss was now, and she made him promise that, above all else, Sable would be safe. That was all his instructions were regarding the babe, and that was all he'd ever found out over the decades.

Lady James acknowledged him, but she didn't speak when he entered the room. There were other people around, many of them relatives that Boo didn't know but could smell the sameness about them. Not that it was any of his business who she had around, but he was curious all the same. He was glad now that he made sure that his lady Sable was sleeping when he'd left, as this looked like it was going to be a very long night. As soon as the others left her, Lady James invited him to have a seat on her hand.

When she put him on the little pillow she'd made just for him, Boo settled down. Not touching the sweet treats that were laid before him until she did, Boo asked her about her health. When she took a chocolate cookie, one of his favorites too, he bit down on a portion of the one she'd been munching on. She ate and drank what she wanted and damn what people told her. Boo laughed when she ate a second cookie with a small glass of sherry.

They both knew she'd not die until she was ready. Not that she was immortal, but when she'd saved his life, then he had hers, she got a bit of his magic in her body and heart that made her live to be nearly three hundred now. Sable was the daughter that she'd had with this marriage.

Sable and her brother Peter had been born twins, Sable the second child in the birth order. But almost as soon as she'd been cleaned up and dressed, she was whisked away and taken to the home she had grown up in.

"You've been watching my daughter very well, Boo. I don't know what I would have done had you not helped me along." He told her that it was his pleasure to serve her. "Be that as it may, you have saved not just her life but mine as well. I wish to repay you for your help."

"I don't need anything, my lady. The young miss doesn't know that I'm about, so I forage into the things that she has around. Flowers are forever fresh in the house she now resides in. There is leftover tea that she leaves that I can have a drink from." Lady James told him that Sable did indeed know he was about. "No. I've been very careful not to show myself around her. I haven't bothered her in all these years."

"Nay, you have not. But she's aware of you. I've been—Sable has my magic. I thought as much when she was born to me. It's the reason she was taken away so quickly and that my husband never knew of her nor the others. To keep her safe from people looking for her." He said that no one bothered her. "They wouldn't. She's powerful, Boo. More so than I am. I don't know how it was that she figured it out, but she has been using her magic, very little of it, since the day she turned two. I'm so very proud of her."

"I am as well. When she was off to higher education, I never once helped her with her exams. She didn't need me to. Sable has won that lottery thing twice now and has invested well. I didn't know what that meant until a few years ago. Nothing more than a toddler when she told her mother to use the numbers she picked out — she knew the correct numbers because of her magic, didn't she?" Lady James — Shirley, as she'd begged him to call her all those years ago — said she knew her parents had needed the income. "So she told her what to play, and they won. Good girl."

"You didn't notice her having magic? I suppose that was the way she wanted it. She is a good girl. She didn't tell her mother so much as she persuaded her to use the numbers." He was very proud of Sable, but he was also ashamed that he'd not noticed it. He told Shirley once again that he was sorry. "There is no reason for you to be sorry, Boo. She never meant for you to notice, and you didn't. However, you were there when she needed you most. When she'd been hurt. Once again, when she'd nearly been kidnapped. Yes, I know of those things and a great many more times that you kept her from being harmed. You did just what I asked you to do, and for that, I'm forever grateful to you. Now, let's get to the reason I've called you here. I need for Sable to be brought here. It's time."

"Time?" Shirley told him she must come home and inherit her estate. And that she must be moving on. "You can't mean that you're to die, my lady. Say that it is something else. I beg of you."

"She's been found, Boo. They know she's out there, and they've narrowed it down to just within miles of them finding her." He asked who they were. "Men and women that would take her apart to see if they can find out what she is. They won't, of course, but they'll try it. For the sake of science, they'll call it, but it will still be murder until she is here again, and I give her what I am. I've no idea what that would be, but I'm sure they'll have some godawful name for it."

"When would you like me to bring her here?

Soon, I would think." Shirley told him the sooner, the better. "I shall bring her here tonight."

"Good. I have several phone calls to make. I've been doing some research, and I do believe I've found the perfect people to care for her. Boo, you'll stay with her, of course. She'll still be in danger while she's with these people." He said he'd be honored. "You've been such a good friend and helper, Boo. I believe I was matched up with the perfect faerie when the lady of the earth sent you to me."

Boo made his way home and was surprised to find Sable awake. She looked directly at him and smiled. Boo went to the couch where she was sitting and asked her if she was all right.

"I'm not sure what you mean by that. I'm not ill, if that's it. I'm also not upset too much. You've been to see someone. Someone that is in need of me to go to them." He told her it was her birth mother. "I don't understand. I do know that the Parkers weren't my parents when I was growing up. However, my birth mother, as far as I know, has had nothing to do with me."

"She has been keeping tabs on you since you

were taken away after you came into this world." Sable nodded but still looked confused. "Lady James is wanting to pass her magic on to you so that when people come to find you, you'll be able to defend yourself."

"My mother will die." It wasn't really a question, but he did nod at her. "So I'm going to meet my mother, and she's going to give me something powerful, then die. What a great way to have a relationship with the one that gave you life. 'Hello, Sable. It's wonderful to meet you. By the way, here's some magic and poof, I'm going to die.' I'm not going."

"But you must." She said she didn't have to do anything she didn't want to. It was then that Lady James appeared in the room. Neither of them said a word but looked at him. "I didn't bring her here."

"I know that." She looked at her mother. "What is it you wish, Lady James? I know someone that can help me keep safe while—"

"They're here. The women I wish for you to go to." Sable stood up when two more people popped into the room. Boo bowed before the three of them, waiting for one of them to tell him that he could stand. "Boo, don't be a nuisance. The men coming for my daughter are near. They — these women are more powerful than even I am. They said you've been found."

"So you're pawning me off to someone else to raise? I don't know if any of you realize this, but I'm a grown woman." The first woman smiled and introduced herself and her sister to her. "Is that supposed to mean something to me? That you're Rain and Storm? It doesn't, in the event, you're going to ask me."

"Touch her now."

Just as her arm was pulled toward her mother, Sable felt something pound her in the chest. Whatever it was, it was making her bleed. Almost as soon as she thought she was going to die, the magic, or whatever power it was, took over her body.

~*~

Garfield watched the woman lying on the bed. He'd been asked to come and talk to her and see if she was his mate. She wasn't. While that did sadden him a bit, he was glad that she'd not been. She looked like a ball buster, and since he most assuredly didn't bust anything but numbers, he watched her body twitch and move with the newfound power she'd been given. Boo entered the room via the window and sat on the side of the bed.

"She's not your mate, then." Garfield told him she was not. "Sad that. She'd make you a good mate, I think."

"I think she'd be too much for me." Boo said she'd be the perfect mate to anyone she was mated to. "I don't suppose you've been practicing this to say to me, have you? I know she'd be a perfect fit in the family, but as for her being my mate, I think we're all right."

Boo was telling him of the things that Sable could do. He wasn't really paying too much attention. The woman on the bed had taken all that. He couldn't seem to take his eyes off her. She was such a beautiful woman.

Sable. Such a pretty name, and it suited her with her long, sable-colored hair. Her fingers were long and well-defined. Even her face looked like a carved goddess. She was, in a word, gorgeous.

Reaching for her hand when it was twitching a great deal, he held it gently in his own to stop her from hitting herself. She'd done it twice now, hit herself in the face while moving around. As soon as he put her hand into his, his entire body seemed to be touched by an electrical wire.

No matter how hard he tried, he couldn't release her hand. Even when she dug her nails into his flesh, Garfield ached with whatever was happening to him. Whatever was going on, two things hit him at once. She was indeed his mate, and she was transferring power to him in great amounts. Then, everything went black.

Waking up, he realized he was in the bed with Sable. She was leaning on one hand and staring down at him. Asking her if she was all right, she told him that she supposed she was but hadn't felt like this before, so she wasn't entirely sure. Then she asked him how he was.

"Like you, I don't know what I'm supposed to feel like right now, so I'll give you that answer later." Moving his head so he could look at her better, Garfield smiled at her. She was even more beautiful with her eyes open. "I've held your hand before to keep you safe. I don't understand. I should have been able to sense that you were my mate. Why did this time make me realize that you were my mate and that you'd do this overpowering thing to me?"

"I had to hide from everyone while my body adjusted to the magic I have. I was assuming I needed to hide from you as well." Garfield told her that made sense. "My mother died. The woman that gave birth to me. I don't know that I saw her pass, but she gave me this magic when she did. Why is there blood on my shirt?"

"You were shot from the window across the street from where you were staying. But the magic kept you from dying and saved you. The people looking for you, I'm assuming you don't know who that would be any more than Boo did." She said she didn't know, but she would find out. "Yes, I believe you will. My sisters-in-law, they're looking into it as well. They're powerful as well." Garfield's eyes were fixated on her mouth. His wolf wanting to claim his mate. "Will you kiss me?"

Sable's face pinked up. "No. Not yet. We may be mates, but I don't know you." He said he understood and he'd try to behave. "Back to what you said before about your sisters-in-law. What makes them think they'll have any more luck with finding them than I did? I've known that someone has been looking for me for some time now, and I've managed to stay off their radar. However, today threw me off guard." Garfield told her that her mother had been protecting her with Boo, but the men were closing in on her location. That was why she'd needed to come to her parent's home. "Yes, so she could give me all that she had and die. I got that part," she said sarcastically. "What I don't understand is why I was sent away in the first place."

"That I do know the answer to. Two powerful beings cannot be in the same place at the same time. You're more powerful than your mother was, so when she came to see you at the house you were at, the men knew where you were. Thus, it was imperative that she give you what she was right away." She nodded and looked at him. "You're very beautiful."

"You should see my sister. Yes, I'm aware of them too. I have a brother and sister that are out there that haven't any idea I'm around. Or, I guess, care." He told her that her brother knew about her. "And? I'm assuming there is a reason that him knowing is a part of this, whatever is happening to me."

"I don't know how he figured it out, but he has been bragging about you. Again, I'm not sure why, but he thought it was funny in some way. These people who were trying to find the magic you would get, they kidnapped your sister and knew it wasn't her magic. She was hurt, I guess, but I don't have a lot of details." He watched her as she seemed to think on that for a moment. "May I ask you some questions?"

She wagged her finger at him. "I'm not ready to kiss you yet. So if that's not your question, go ahead." He laughed, and she glared at him. "I wasn't joking around."

"I know that. I just found it a little funny that you are not allowing me to kiss you yet." She frowned at him again. "What are you? Boo hasn't any idea just so you know. I'm assuming something powerful, but I don't know what you are."

"Unlucky?" She shrugged. "I don't know either. I can do all this crazy shit that keeps me in money. Not that I need all the money in the world, I guess, but my foster parents had money problems from the moment I came to them. I guess before that even, but I helped them out." She explained about the lottery money.

"After that, they invested well, thanks to my being able to see what stocks and things were going to do well, and I could persuade or make them invest."

"I'm an investment broker. I, for the most part, do it for the family. Since we've been around for a good long time, we've been able to put some money into accounts that needed it when times were tough. Also, help out different charities when that was needed." Sable said she did the same thing. "I don't know if you're aware of this or not, but you're an immortal. A true one in which you cannot be killed. You can be hurt, but you'll never die from it."

"I'm assuming I can heal quickly too." He nodded. "All right. I'm ready to kiss you now. But no funny business. I just need a kiss."

"You need a hug too. I can feel your stress." She said she was dealing with it. "I'll take you up on the kiss later if you would allow me to hold you. Your stress is making my wolf a little nervous."

"Too much going on right now for me to process. I can feel your wolf too. He is antsy." She laid her head on his chest and her hand on his belly. "I can feel him there. I can hear him purring too. I had no idea that wolves purred."

"He's trying to lure you into sleep. You need it." She yawned and said she did. "Rest now, Sable, and we'll talk more later. All right?"

Sable was asleep in a few minutes. Her body no longer twitched, but she did dig her fingers into his belly a couple of times. Still, he held her. Holding her had the same effect on him. Relaxing enough to sleep by her beating heart, Garfield joined her in slumber.

Chapter 1

"I think that I said this before. I'm a grown assed woman, and I can and will make my own decisions as to what happens to me from now on. If you have any advice? Well, I'll take that into consideration when I'm deciding. But for now, I want the three of you to get out of...where am I anyway?" Rain told her where she was. "All right. I'd like it if you were to please leave me alone for a bit in your house so that I can think. Christ, my head is spinning with all the books ever written being downloaded into my head all at once. I just need to think."

Rain moved to the door and stood on the threshold with Storm right next to her. "We can do that, Sable, but you have to be aware that you're in danger." Sable said she knew that, and she could even feel the presence of someone looking for her, but she needed to settle. "The men that came for you this time have been dealt with, but that won't stop them from coming again. They're a large group of people wanting to tear you apart."

"Literally, I'm assuming." Neither woman so much as blinked at her when she spoke. "I'm not worried about them at the moment. I haven't any idea why but I'm just not. It could be because of the two of you. Or it might have something to do with Garfield being around. It could be that I'm just overstressed with shit that I didn't get a chance to ask about. I haven't any idea, but for now, I just need to get my shit together and think. And I can't do that with everyone constantly hovering over me."

Storm nodded. "I know I don't have to tell you this, but for my own peace of mind, I'm going to say it. Please don't leave the house. Not even to reach out to people. Until Rain and I figure out where these people are coming from, I'd rather no one know that you're here." Sable told Storm that she'd not do anything to harm her family. "Thank you for that. We'd only spoken to the woman, Lady James, once before we were summoned to go to help you the day that those people found you. I have no idea why but I have a feeling that's the way that she planned things. To make it so that there was no way you could turn her down with her giving you her magic. Rain and I are looking into some things for you and for us, I guess. Things aren't what they seem. Also, the Parkers? The people that you lived with? We're not able to locate them either. It's like they were never born."

That gave Sable pause. She had lived with the Parkers until she'd been eighteen, never bothering them after that but sending them cards occasionally and to meet up with them during the holidays. Now they were gone? Thinking about the couple, she carefully let her mind search for them. Sable's heart ached when she touched on what she was looking for.

"They're dead. Both of them." Storm told her that she was sorry for that. "They were killed the day that…no, not killed but were destroyed the day that those people came looking for me. I'm assuming because I have no way of knowing that those people did it. Changing their names too could have been a way for them to keep me safe too. They were the Hanson's before I was brought to them. Does that help?"

"Yes. I can do a search on them now that I have their names." Rain smiled at her then and told her what she'd been able to figure out already. "I've been able to find out about why they were chosen to take you now. They had put in for an adoption for a child, and you were who came up on the list for them. Or so they were told. Boo, your little faerie fixed the paperwork so that they'd be the ones to take you. He made sure that they got you because they had nothing to do with magic in their lives, and they weren't wealthy. I'm to understand that you helped them out with their money situation when you were smaller."

"I was two at the time. I knew that they weren't my real parents by then and wanted to make sure, for whatever reason they took me in, that none of us had to go without. The lottery was the fastest and the easiest way for them to get the money that was sorely needed, as well as make it so that we had a roof over our heads. They were renters at that time and were set to lose everything when money was so tight." Storm asked her how she'd figured out the numbers. "At that time, I had no idea where the winning numbers came from in my mind. But they worked. After the winnings were given to them, I also helped with investments for the family. Myself as well, I guess. But they never put it together with me having magic. I don't think so, anyway. After I turned ten, it was much easier for me to get around them. Not in a bad way, but I could help them with money in ways that wouldn't have drawn attention to any of us."

"Someone figured out something. I'm not saying it was the money. Because as far as I can see in your life, you never flaunted nor did your parents their wealth. But something alerted the people where you were." Sable said that she'd help them if she could figure out things. "We're both aware that you've been given a great deal of magic. My understanding of it is that you are also learning how to use it."

"Yes. That's what I need to settle in my head. It's not as bad as it was before, but it's still a constant bombardment of information that I'm dealing with." It was Storm that told her that they'd let her get used to it. "Thanks. I mean, I've only been asking for the time for about an hour or two now." Storm laughed.

"I like you, Sable. You're outspoken and a bitch. But I like you. I think you're going to fit well into this family." Sable said nothing as the two women left her. Once the door was closed behind them, she lay out on the floor and closed her eyes.

Sorting out the magic wasn't going to be easy with the amount of it she had. Using her considerable magic to seal off the room from anyone that might be looking for a lot of magic like she had, Sable shoved all the magic from her mind and let it surround her in the room. Using the space of the room as a holding place for the magic until she could put it in some kind of order. Lying on the floor like she was, it felt like she had more room to work with.

She didn't know how long she lay there working before she realized that she wasn't alone in the room. Garfield had joined her at some point and had quietly laid down beside her. When she asked him if he was all right, he told her that he wasn't sure.

"Whatever you're doing is helping me as well. My head was splitting with all the things that were circling around in there, so when I felt you easing into this, I guess you could call it, I knew that I had to be with you. And so you know, I just appeared here when I thought of being with you." She asked him if it had freaked him out. "That seems such a mild term for how I felt when I ended up here. But once I got over that, pretty quickly, I might add, my mind began to feel better the longer I laid here."

They didn't speak again as she worked the magic. Garfield was so still like he knew that if he became a distraction, she'd toss him out. Smiling to herself, she knew that while she could actually toss him out of the room, she'd not do that to him. There was something so very calming about him being so close to her that she didn't want to mess with that feeling from him.

At some point, she must have dozed off. Once she saw that all the magic in the room was gone, now, she supposed in her mind, she sat up. Lying back down again, careful not to do anything too fast again, she looked over at Garfield when he said her name. Even though it was spoken softly, she turned to look at him.

"You're so beautiful, Sable." She felt her face heat up in embarrassment. "Once you fell asleep, I was able to finish up what you started. It was easier because I'd been watching you do it, but I think that we need to rest a bit more before we get up and start moving around. I tried to get up earlier, and I decided, or at least my body did, that lying here on the floor is better than face-planting myself and more than likely hurting my body in some way."

"It's like it's all too much for me." Garfield told her that was how he'd felt too. Overwhelmed. "I can put us in the bed if that would be more comfy."

"Being anywhere you are is comfy for me, but you're right. The bed would be better. By the way, I've spoken to my family about what is going on. They're going to let us rest up a bit before they come at us all at once. I think you've met some of my family." She said that all she'd met so far was Rain and Storm. "Yes, well, they're the scariest of the bunch. Edwin, who is mated to Storm, is the alpha of the wolf pack that we're a part of. My brother Tony and Jana are their seconds. I'm not sure what that could mean in the way of all the magic that we all have, but he and Jana are there for him and Storm if they need them."

She put them in the bed so that they'd be more comfortable. She hadn't realized until then that she was stiff from the hardness beneath her back. As soon as they pulled a light blanket over them, Sable felt exhausted again and closed her eyes. Someone nudged at her mind just as she was feeling like she was dreaming.

"Hello, my darling daughter. This is the only way that I can speak to you without us destroying the world I've come to love. You're much more lovely than I could have imagined you to be." Sable asked her why she'd gotten the magic and not her firstborn. "Ah, there is nothing wrong with your thinking, is there? She didn't get the magic because she would flitter it away on silly things. Things that would only benefit herself and those she thinks of as friends. She has none in the event you were going to ask."

"What about Peter? He was born before me. I'm the youngest of your children, and while I should have gotten some of your magic, I have it all. Please explain yourself. I'd like to understand this before I start using it. Please." The being, her biological mother, she supposed, laughed. "I don't think this is the least bit funny. I was happy with...no, I wasn't happy, but I had a life before this."

"And you will have a better life now. Peter. Let me think of a way to tell you this without having you — no hope for it. I just have to tell it like it is. Peter is the one that has sold you off to the men and women who search for you even now, I believe. I'm not positive how it was that he found out about you, but he is the one that would have you taken by them. He stood to make a great deal of money, but alas, he's going to have to start over as Rain and Storm have protected you somewhat from them. You did a lot to keep yourself safe too." She asked why. As she'd only just gotten her magic. "Oh, but you had more than him before you took all that I have. I don't know the whole of it as to why he was set on selling you to them, but I will."

"Before it's too late, I'm hoping." Again, her mother laughed. "There are a few things that I have to know before we finish speaking. Garfield is my mate. He's a good man from an extraordinary family. I wish no harm to come to any of them. I will kill whoever comes after them to get to me."

"And you can, child. Kill whoever comes for you and your mate. Peter nor Belinda, your older sister, are true immortals. They can be killed, as can your father.

It is written, as I'm sure you understand, that there are no rules pertaining to the harm that any of you cause, the ones that come for you and those that you hold dear to your heart. That would mean the Griffins, as well as anyone else that you wish. So you may and will, I believe, be able to kill your blood relatives as easily as the people coming for you. Your powers and that of Garfield are that strong." She asked if she could see the future where she did have to kill one of her family members. "I cannot. But I do know that they will die trying to kill you."

"Because I'm stronger than them?" Mother said that it was more than that. She wasn't just stronger than them magically but simply smarter than them. "It's doubtful that anyone would think them very smart if they tangled with a being that is obviously stronger magically than them. But I don't know a lot about them. Are they that stupid?"

"Peter decided that since you were his sister, you'd just come to him willingly to give over the magic you have. Simply because you're younger than him. Even before you took what I had, you were stronger than him. He thought, as you did, that being the only male, he should have been given it all. And, he thinks that your sister Belinda should have been put to death as well as you because what use is a woman when there is magic to be had." Sable had to laugh at the logic or the lack of logic that her brother had. "I don't know where he thought he came from, being that he thinks all women should be killed, but that's his mindset. What he intends to use the magic for, you might ask? To kill off every female born. I'm sure you can understand how that is going to be not just difficult to do but also something that will have consequences forever forward."

"Okay, yes, he's stupid. What about Belinda? What is her play in having me killed? I'm sure that you've got an idea." Mother told her that Belinda was happy just being rich. She could care less about the magic. "Shallow then. I don't mean to sound rude or anything, but you raised yourself a great group of children. Unless, of course, you had very little to do with their upbringing as you did me."

"You're correct. I'd like to say that their father made them what they are today. But he was just as absent from their lives as I was. Not that he was a terrible person to me or the children. However, he did make it so his children had everything they wanted, whether they needed it or not. So an endless supply of money and no consequences when they screw up made them intolerable to anyone and everything. They've screwed up plenty." Sable corrected her. "All right. They fucked up plenty. And they have too. A great deal more than I think I'm aware of. And yes, Belinda is just as bad as her brother. She has money and has no trouble tossing that around to get what she wants. And if that didn't work, she'd resort to stealing whatever it was that she didn't have and someone else did."

Sable didn't know what to say about this information. She knew that it would be helpful if she — not if but when she was confronted by her biological family, but right now, all she could see was that she'd been the only one that had turned out all right. At least, she thought so.

She and her mother talked for a bit more. Information on the others was helpful, but she wasn't sure what to do about them as yet. Sable thought that if they left her alone, she would leave them alone. But she wouldn't stand for them coming around to cause trouble. No one needed that shit.

When she woke this time, she was alone in the big bed. Sable remembered at the last second not to reach out for anyone. Getting up, she took a long hot shower and then dressed herself. While she knew whose house she was in, she had no idea what to expect when she left the room.

Going down the long staircase, Sable followed the voices of young children who were having a snack with the cook. Sitting with them, Sable got to meet the Griffin children and was delighted to see that they were nothing like the rich pricks of her own family. They were polite young kids that enjoyed being a family. She could get used to this, she thought.

~*~

Garfield wasn't positive about what he was looking at. However, he did know that he'd been looking at the same page for the last few minutes and didn't have a clue as to what the entire thing was about. More than likely an hour or so. But his mind wouldn't center on what he was looking at. It wanted to go back to the conversation that he'd had with Sable when she'd told him about the magic they both had.

"The two of us are indestructible. I mean that in a literal sense too." Then she told him about her biological family and how they were immortal; however, they could be killed by something hitting their heart or removing their heads. "I didn't think about it being a separate thing what we are to them, but I think it'll work out the best for us when they do come around." Garfield agreed with his mate.

His mate. Sable Parker was just down the hall from him right now, talking to Storm and Rain. He could have stayed there with them, talking too, but he had a million and a half things to get caught up on. Watching the three of them argue about magic wasn't getting him anywhere close to being finished. The paperwork that he told Edwin would be finished yesterday wasn't even half finished, and he'd yet to review the end reports with it.

"You do realize that the longer you sit there, the less you're going to get done, don't you?" He looked at his brother Tony when he spoke. "Look. I've been to see what is going on with them. They're doing nothing but talking about how much more magic one has than the other. Sort of like they're measuring their dicks or something. If you wanted to be there with them, I'm sure that they'd not mind."

"Which one has the most magic?" Tony said he wasn't going to speculate on that question. "I can understand that. Having the most magic or not, the three of them are too powerful to piss off. Even just one of them is scary enough."

"The good thing to remember is that they can't kill us. I'm sure if we pushed hard enough, they'd hurt us. I keep telling myself over and over that they can't kill me. It gets me through my days." Tony asked him what he would do if they were pissed at him. "Hide. Not that I think it would do me any good. But I'd do my best to hide from them until they didn't remember what I'd done to upset them."

Tony laughed. "I think you have the right idea. Sable is holding her own if that matters to you." Garfield said she scared him a little. "Yeah, me too. At least I'm not mated to the other two, where I have to worry all the time. I'd be scared out of my mind each time I opened my mouth to see if I screwed up, and they're going to knock me three ways from Sunday."

"I'm worried about that too, without saying a word. I keep telling myself that they can read my mind better than I can. That in and of itself is enough to make you wear an aluminum foil hat all the time" Tony and Garfield both laughed hard at that. "But seriously though, it is scary to have so much power coming from one family. And now that we have Sable around, there is no telling what sort of trouble we might be getting into."

"Trouble should heed the warnings and hide out too. Because you know as well as I do that if one of us or them is in trouble, they're all going to come to help out. I would rethink everything if I were thinking of coming to this family for anything other than good news." The two of them sat there talking for a while, and Garfield did feel better about his day so far.

When Edwin showed up, they included him in their speculations on who had the most power. He said that he was going to stay out of it simply because he, like them, was afraid of the answer. But he did have something for them to talk about.

"The pack school is in need of a few things that I think we can provide for them. One of which are they need new computers. While they can afford them, I think we can figure out a way for them to get a good price on a lot of them. They're also talking about teaching some classes—for humans too—for the elderly to learn how to use one. Not just on how to look things up but paying bills as well as ordering groceries too. I know the local schools are doing that now rather than depending on someone to come in weekly and order the food stuff for the building. To be honest, I hadn't ever thought of how they get food into the school system before." Garfield asked him if he thought it just appeared when they needed it. "I haven't any idea what I thought. But that happens at our house, so perhaps it would be a good thing to have happen at the schools."

"We all know that wouldn't work. We tried that before. There has to be accountability with not just the money that is coming in, but also there are businesses that depend on the income from the schools when they order from them. It always has some kind of trickle-down issues when we try to use magic to help out in a way that saves money for large businesses. And a school would be counted in that." The women joined them in the room then, and all three of them stood up.

He was the only one that didn't cover his balls when they stood beside them. Garfield kissed Sable on the mouth when she grinned at him. "We were just talking about school systems and the lack of funding for some things. The pack house has an idea about adult learning with computers. Beyond what they have going on now at the center. Ordering grocery lists and things like that."

"Would that be a school system issue? I mean, if they're not involved, why is this a school board issue?" Tony asked Rain what she meant. "Well, I mean, adults imply that kids won't be learning with them or around when they are being taught this idea you have. It would seem to me that if kids aren't involved, then it would be easier to donate the computers that they need. Rather than going through all the red tape a school board and system would require. Especially if it wasn't held at the school. Then there is the red tape for all of that going on too." Garfield asked her what she would do. With a shrug, she told him. "Hold the adult classes at a neutral location. That way, people won't know where your pack is at all times, but also no one will have to travel through the wooded areas to get there. If you do this in town, I think you'll have a good deal more people show up too. And pack people can be transported there in a bus or something. Win-win for everyone."

They spoke about what could be done for the schools, both the pack and human school to help them out. With Edwin being the pack leader, it was easier to run it by him first. He was all for the idea but was glad they had suggested that it be off-site for the pack.

"Like she explained about them finding where we live is a good enough reason for them not being on pack land. You never know when someone is going to get a burr up their ass and come after us. I like this idea a great deal. In fact, I think we can work out something on a building downtown. We, as a family, own a great many of them. I could donate that to the city." Storm said that might not be a good thing. They'd take advantage of his generosity if he were willing to donate a building for the older people, why not donate a pool for the kids. Or upgrade the school's football fields. "Yes, you're right. I should have remembered the last time this happened when we donated a lot of money and donations to a cause. That same thing happened exactly as you said it. I think I'll just rent it to them for like fifty years at a reasonable rent, and that should keep me out of their loop."

"I doubt it, but you can always think that." They were all laughing when they decided that they were going to grill out. Mom and dad were going to join them with dessert later, and Garfield couldn't have been happier about it.

The weather was perfect, but he was noticing that some of the trees were turning already. He knew that it was mid-August right now, but he wasn't happy about the summer ending. He wanted it to last all year round. But winter brought on Thanksgiving and Christmas, and he was looking forward to that as well. Having a mate would be an amazing addition to all the celebrations for the entire family, Garfield thought.

Chapter 2

Peter was pissed off. Not that it wasn't his usual mood of late, but he was pissed off because he couldn't find his mother, and his father was about as useless as the fucking cat that he pampered to death. The cat had to weigh about twenty pounds and did nothing more than walk to his food dish and back. But his mother wasn't around.

Pacing the long hallway to build up enough steam so that when he saw Belinda again, he'd be able to knock her around a bit more than he usually did. Not that it happened all that often. Belinda could and would take him down if he didn't get a good punch or two in before she did. The last time she'd come out of her stupor, he'd spent five days in bed nursing not only a broken nose but also she'd bloodied his ear as well.

"Stupid bitch." He thought about the other sister. His twin, he supposed. Where the hell was she? Liking how much more angry he was getting thinking about the twin, he worked himself up quicker by making up stories about her that he thought about. "Fucking cunt. Where are you?"

He only knew about her because one afternoon, he'd been sneaking around his mother's office when he found the certificate that announced that he'd been born. It wasn't a birth certificate like his human friends had but an announcement that declared him being brought into the world by his parent. It was fancy looking, too, with scrolled letters and such. Then at the bottom of the safety box, he found an actual birth certificate for a female child, but there was no name on it.

No parents' names. Nothing that he could see as to why his mother had kept it. But the date and time of her birth were a match to his but for twenty-two minutes after his time of birth, had him going to his mother and asking about it.

"What were you doing in my office?" He asked her what that had to do with the certificate. "What were you doing snooping around in my office, Peter? You know that it's off-limits to you. I'm guessing that you had to break into my office, not to mention the safe where this was, to get to it. Why would you do that? Nothing in *my* safe concerns you."

"You're not answering my question. I demand that you tell me why —" It was the first time anyone had ever hit him before. And her slapping him on the cheek sent him to the floor, where she dared him to get up from. "You hit me. Why would you think that was going to be all right with me? Don't ever do that again."

But she had. When he stood up and drew back his fist to show her why she wasn't to hit him again, she slapped him again and again until his face was hurting from it. Taking a step back from her, hoping she'd not reach him, his mother hit him in the face with her fist. It was a week before he went to her again about the certificate, and she took it from him and burned it in the fire. Now he had nothing to go on. Not even if he wanted to take it to his father to get answers from him.

However, it didn't stop him from looking into things. It didn't do him much good. No one was talking about the female child, nor would they even acknowledge his questions when he put them to the staff. He hated them all.

Having his anger right where he wanted it. Peter went to the door of his sister's bedroom. It was time for her to get her ass beaten. While he didn't know why he wanted to hurt her today, he just knew that if he didn't, there was going to be a lot of deaths of faeries around the castle.

Lifting his foot up to knock the door open, he focused all of his energy and anger into his foot. When he could feel like he was stronger than anyone in the place, he was going to slam his foot to the right of the knob.

The door opened just as he was touching the door with his anger. As he fell forward, the momentum of his propulsion giving him nothing to stop his motion going forward, he hit the floor with his face. Not only did he hear his nose break, but the pain of it went down to his feet and back up again. The second bounce, this was to the rest of his body, was too much. Passing out, he hoped to Christ that someone would take care of him nicely while he was out cold.

Opening his eyes to the brightness of the light that was overhead, Peter looked around as easily as he could. His face hurt badly, and he could feel the bandages around his head. He wanted to find someone to tell him what was going on, but right now, it was difficult for him to work up enough spit to even pry his mouth open.

Listening to his surroundings was all he had left to do. There didn't seem to be a call button for him to push, and yelling was out of the question for the moment. Besides, he thought for sure that someone had locked him in the bed. Not only could he not move his legs and feet, but he was having trouble just being able to move his head around to look.

It only just occurred to him that he was in the hospital. Where, he didn't know. There was one near the house where he lived, but he'd never had the occasion to go there. Being immortal and his mother able to fix everything else, it had never occurred to him to go and check the place out. But he was going to make changes as soon as he took over someday. The place was a dump.

The walls in this part of the hospital were a drab green. Why anyone would think that it was a color to be conducive to getting better was beyond him. They needed to be blinding colors. Reds and blues like you would encounter in neon. Peter loved color in his brightest forms.

He heard the click-click of heels coming down the hall. It was either someone that worked the streets or a very stupid nurse. However, Peter did think that going into a profession that would get you covered in blood and puke made one stupid. As soon as the curtain was thrown back, he nearly sobbed to see his sister standing there. Then he remembered that he was only here because she'd opened her door rather than let him bust it in.

"What the fuck do you want? I'm pissed at you, Belinda. You fucked me over, and don't think that I won't—"

"Oh, goody. You're awake. Finally." He asked Belinda where he was. "In the hospital. All though, I think you could have figured that out on your own by now. You've been here for three days, and I was beginning to think you were never going to wake up so that I could tell you the news. I want you to know that they did everything they could to help you with your injuries, but you hit the floor much too hard for them to save you from walking again. I'm sorry about that. No, I won't lie to you. I don't care for you at all, Peter, so I'm sort of glad that you won't be able to terrorize anyone, especially me, anymore."

"What are you talking about?" She told him that when he'd hit his body on her bedroom floor, he'd broken his back. Thus paralyzing himself from the waist down. "No. You're lying to me. Why would you be so fucking cruel about something like that? There is nothing wrong with my body. You hear me? And even if there is, it can be fixed. I'm an immortal. Did you hear me? I won't put up with these lies."

"I think everyone heard you, Peter. Now. I have some other news for you. And I haven't any idea why this makes me so happy — more than likely because you've been a shit since you took your first breath. But you're not only unable to walk, but you also have a colostomy bag that needs to be emptied of your shit twice a day. Not to mention your piss is just draining out of you all the time into a little baggie to your side. You can't have sex either, I'm thrilled to tell you. Nothing works below the waist. Remember me telling you that?" Belinda laughed. "I don't know what I find funnier. You being out of commission for the rest of your long and wheelchair-bound life or the fact that you're going to need constant care by someone that will pick you up and carry you around like a little baby. Like you are most of the time anyway."

"This isn't funny. I want you to find mother and have her come and heal me. She can do it." Belinda looked so sad in that second that he found himself wanting to lash out at her even more. But that didn't negate the fact that she had to help him in any way possible, as he was the rightful person to take over the kingdom when his mother passed away. "Where is she anyway? I've been trying to find her for the last couple of days."

"She's gone, Peter. Mother decided it was time for her to go, and she just faded away. She died. I can't believe that you didn't feel it when it happened. The ground shook, and it started raining terribly. Didn't you feel a thing?" He had but thought it was when he'd been fucking one of the chamber maids, and he'd come hard. Then it occurred to him what Belinda had been saying. "Mother passed on about four days ago. I know it was before you tried to hurt me. That I know for sure. But when you were hurt, I couldn't remember the date she left us. Isn't that funny?"

"Nothing that spews from your mouth is funny. But I am glad for one thing. I have her powers. Holy shit, I can heal myself." Before she could tell him about the rule about not being able to benefit from his own magic, which wasn't going to apply to him now that he was in charge, he snapped his fingers twice as he watched his legs. Even after several tries, nothing happened to make his legs move again. "I can't move them. I can't feel anything, either. What happened? Did you do this to me? So help me, Belinda, I'll kill you if you've done this to me. Fix this."

"I can't fix it. I wouldn't even if I could. But I can't. Nor did you get mother's powers. I didn't, either. So whatever happened to her, her powers aren't with either of us anymore. I've noticed, too, that father is getting older by the hour. Like he's fading himself."

She was babbling on about the castle fading as well, and the flowers were dying. He told her to shut up and fix him. "How? Do you want me to toss you out of the bed there and command you to walk? I. Can't. Fix. You. Dumbass." Then she stood up, and he told her to sit down.

"I'm not finished talking to you. You'll sit right there and tell me what your plans are in getting my legs working again." She just left him there. Like he wasn't talking to her. "I'm sick to death of everyone treating me as if I'm nothing, Belinda. Now that I'm in charge, you'll see what I can do."

He heard her laughter as it faded from him. Moving the small sheet completely off his legs, he looked at them. They looked fine to him. Concentrating all his focus on his toes, he was covered in sweat when he realized that he couldn't even make his toes wiggle and that his sister might be right on this. But he'd never admit that to her.

"I'm just in shock, that's all." He told himself over and over that it had nothing to do with his fall and that his sister was paying people to make him not be able to move. "I'll show her what's what when I'm out of here. And I'm going to find my mother's magic too. Whoever has it is going to be in for a lot of pain when I find them."

Peter laid back on the bed when the nurse came in to talk to him. Ignoring her for the pain meds she was giving him, Peter let it settle over him like a warm buzz. She'd come back, she told him, but he didn't care. He was thinking and planning. Just the way he needed to do right now.

~*~

Going to the front of the house to see who was there for her, Sable saw the woman a few seconds before she made a noise to alert her that she was watching her. While she didn't have much of an idea who she might be, she thought that she was looking at her older sister. When she turned toward her when Sable asked if she could help her, all doubts of her being anyone else but Belinda flew out the window.

"You're Sable, my sister." Nodding, she made her way to the other woman while holding onto the baskets of fruit firmly in her hands. There was no way that she was going to touch someone that she didn't know. Sable had learned that the hard way. "I've come here to — well, to get to know you, I guess. Also, I want to let you know that you don't have to worry about Peter anymore. He's been injured recently and won't be able to come near anyone again."

"Should I have been worried about him?" They sat down on the front porch as Belinda told her she had every reason to be afraid of Peter as he was off his noodle. "I see. I don't, but being off his noodle, I'm assuming that you might well have had something to do with that?"

Her laughter had her smiling. "I think that he's always been off his rocker. I haven't any idea what was done to him or for him to think he was better than everyone else. I would like to blame it on my father, but he was never a part of our lives. I guess he's your father as well." Sable told her that she wasn't sure what to think of him as. "I guess I can understand that as well. You've been living elsewhere since you were born, I'm assuming."

"Yes. With the Parkers. They were killed recently. I didn't think to blame one of you guys, but I'm guessing now that I should assume it was Peter." She said that she'd heard about them and figured that he'd done it as well. "Would you happen to know why he'd do that to an innocent couple?"

"He wanted information about you. And I'm assuming they didn't give them anything, and he killed them. From what I can tell, he didn't know your name or anything much about you. However, I knew a great deal. You see, I found my mother's notebooks before she died. Actually, I was just a teenager when I found them. I knew about you for a long time, but since mother had decided that you didn't belong with us, I'd not do a thing about it either. I think she knew that I had read them, but she never said anything to me about not doing it. So I would go to her room and read them over to sort of keep up on things in your life." Sable asked if she could read them. "I wish I could tell you that it would be wonderful if you did. But when she left this world, the books — all of them disappeared as well. Not even the one I had been reading in my room is around anymore. Perhaps you have them now that you have her power?"

"It would never have occurred to me to look for them. I will now, of course. What else can you tell me about your life with her?" She smiled at her, and Sable couldn't help but smile back at her. "Why do I have the feeling that I had the better of the two of our lives."

"You may well have. Living with them in the magical home wasn't easy. Mostly because of Peter, but our father didn't play any kind of role in our lives either. It wasn't like he was abusive or a drunk. He was just out of touch with us. Even mother. I think, and this is just me, I think father didn't want to be married to mother because she had all this magic and he didn't. That too might have played a role in Peter's life too."

"I can see that. I've been magical all my life. Not as much as I am now, but I've been able to do things for myself that others might not have been able to help me with. I could always heal quickly. I've never been sick where it would put me down. Did you have those perks growing up?" Belinda said that they did but in a very small way. "Why is it that Peter is hurt? I'm assuming that he did something that you had to take him to task about."

"No. Well, I guess indirectly. He was outside my bedroom door, working up enough energy to beat my door down, then beat me. It, as you might call it, was a pastime for him to hurt me. He's been a jackass all his life, acting like everyone should bow down before him and pay homage. I didn't. I doubt very much anyone did, to be honest with you. However, that didn't stop him from demanding it." She wasn't sure why but Sable believed Belinda in that. "He's been paralyzed by a fall that injured his back permanently. After he is released from the hospital, he'll need to go into nursing care to keep him alive. I foresee that not lasting very long. Not that he can or will care for himself, but he won't want people around to make him feel less of a man. He also thinks that when our mother faded, he should have gotten the magic she had because of him being her only male son. You have it, don't you? I can almost taste it on you."

"I did get it. As did my mate." Belinda congratulated her. She wasn't sure if it was the mate or the magic, but she let it go. "I haven't any idea what I am. I have a sister-in-law that is married to my husband's brother, that doesn't know what I am either. Storm, I think you've met is twin to Rain. They have a great deal of magic all on their own. The story goes that they are the result of magic being untapped but passed down from generation to generation until they were able to use it. They're very powerful, the two of them. And in turn, so are the people around them as they have shared."

"I don't know why but I assumed that you would know as soon as the magic came to you who you are. Our mother was the sister to the lady of the earth. Grace. They, too, were born as twins but stayed together throughout their lives. Grace, our aunt, is older than our mother was by about ten minutes. And as she was older, Aunt Grace was given the bulk of the magic in order to take care of the earth and all its creatures. Mother helped when she was asked to, but that wasn't all that often. Not that she was any less powerful, but they were good and kind to each other and helped all those that needed it." Sable asked if she was close to Grace. "Not especially. I mean, I know her. I've been to her palace a few times, but I'd not say we were close. I believe with all my heart that it had more to do with her being super busy than anything to do with me. Also, I don't think she cared all that much for our father or brother. When we were all together for some party or something, as you can imagine, Peter would cause trouble. Bitching about one thing or another that would get us sent home in disgrace. After a while, there were no more invites for the family and mother would go and see her when she was asked. That didn't sit well with father either just so you know."

"I would imagine that mother didn't have a good life all the way around. I still wonder why she sent me away." She told her that it was to keep her safe from Peter. "Did she believe that they'd hurt me?"

"Yes." When she didn't say anything else, Sable let it go too. When Belinda stood up, she did as well. "I must be going. I'd like to come and visit you again if you'd not mind. I've enjoyed this more than I can tell you."

"I have as well. Thank you for coming to see me." When she walked away from her without another word, Sable sat down on the rocker that she had been sitting in. She had no idea why but she didn't trust Belinda. It wasn't until she walked away that the feeling hit her. Whatever she was up to, Sable was going to be on the lookout for Belinda and her ways. There was something so very…well, wrong about all this. Now that she was alone, questions popped into her head that she'd not thought of before while visiting with her.

If she knew about her, why hadn't she come to see her before now? Why was she being so friendly after all this time? Other questions went around in her head that painted Belinda in a dark place. One thing was certain, she wasn't going to trust any of them until she had facts. And having just the little information that she had now, being niece to Grace, the mother of the earth, would be something she was going to check into as soon as possible.

Finding Storm and Rain proved to be a little more difficult than she had thought it would. Rain came to her when she reached out to her, and Storm told her that she'd be there soon. She was looking over some paperwork that had been given to her. As soon as they were all three in the living room, with scones and tea, Sable told them everything that had been said between her and her sister.

"You don't believe her." Sable told Rain that it wasn't that she didn't believe her. It was more that she didn't trust what she was telling her. "Okay, that, to me, is the same thing. So you have this sister and brother you've had nothing to do with. Now all of a sudden, they turn up, and you're not good with that. I have to admit, I'd not be good with that either. It would have been easier on me had she not just shown up. She needed to have made some other—come to think of it. How the hell did she know where you lived now? It's not like you've advertised the fact that you and Garfield have made any sort of announcement. For all she knew, you could have been at the Parker home still. Yeah, I'm agreeing with you on the not trusting stuff. Also, what do you actually know about any of them, for that matter? Even your parents? Nothing. Would you mind if I had a look around her head?"

"No, go ahead." Jana, another sister-in-law, showed up just as they were making plans to see Peter. Not that he'd see them, but it would be nice to see if anything she said about him was true. Jana suggested sending a faerie to have a look around, and no one would be none the wiser about it. "Great idea. Maybe whoever you send can have a look at my father as well as Belinda."

"Yes, I like that. We'll send out a few so that they can take turns gathering information. I don't know how long that would take, but it would be helpful to all of us if we had something more to go on." It was then that Storm asked her if she'd called to her aunt. "Do you think she really is my aunt? I mean, I haven't ever thought of someone like her in existence. I suppose that's the point. That's how she would stay safe."

"Call to her." Sable looked at Rain when she spoke. "What harm can it do for you to call her here or even to speak to her if you need information? If it turns out that she's not related to you, then what are you out? Nothing. Just call to her and see what sort of information, if any, she can give to you."

"I'll do it." They ended up in the back yard and her barefooted, standing in the grass. She didn't know why she went along with that part of calling her, but she was going to do it. "Grace, Queen of all the earth, would you mind coming to me when you have time? I just have a few questions."

A bright spot appeared almost as soon as she was finished speaking. As it grew bigger, forming into a woman, Sable began to have her doubts about this being a good idea. She knew nothing about this woman or her powers. As soon as she was fully a person she could speak to, her wings, bright with the light that showed through them, spread out behind her.

"Hello. Oh my, you look so much like your mother when she was small." Sable told her that she didn't know her mother. "No. You'd not. I didn't know of you either, or I might well have intervened on your behalf. Oh, but we'll have fun now, won't we? My name, as you know, is Grace. I'm sorry, but I don't know your name at all, but I do accept you as my blood relative, daughter to my twin, niece to me. I'm so happy to know you."

"Sable Parker Griffin, mate to Garfield Griffin. That's about all the lineage that I know for sure about. Other than you just telling me that I'm your niece." She asked her why she had her doubts. "I've been hearing about my biological family. Mostly from Belinda. I'm not sure that I trust her all that much."

"You shouldn't trust any of your biological family. Well, you could have trusted Shirley, your mother and me now that we've met. But the other three? No. I'd not trust them for as far as you can toss them. Without magic, anyway. I'm so happy to meet you, Sable. And I'm so happy that you're now with one of the greatest creations of all time. My wolves."

Sable asked if she'd received her mother's magic. "You did. All of it. And a bit more from me. How about we have a nice talk when the family gets together. I have information to impart to you and the others. You'll need it all, I'm afraid, in dealing with the others."

They set up a meeting for them to come to dinner the next night. While she didn't have any idea what she might expect from this talk, she felt better just knowing that she had a trust with Grace that she didn't have with Belinda. Whatever came of this, she was going to go into it with an open mind. And a gun. She wasn't totally stupid about family.

Chapter 3

Garfield was ready to call it a night. He'd been on several conference calls since this morning, and he didn't think half of them didn't go in the client's favor. When he invested in a project, he wanted results. Not excuses. The one project he'd been so excited about turned out to be nothing more than a red hole of money being stuffed into it rather than the money maker he and the client had been hoping for.

"I tell you, Mr. Griffin, if you could just give me another ten grand, I know that we can get this up and running the correct way." Garfield pointed out that they'd already given them enough money to have had it going. "I had to see to some bills that were piling up around me. I couldn't lose my house and car, now could I? What would I have to get back and forth to work."

Before Garfield got a chance to answer him, his lovely mate joined him in the office. He'd been talking to her off and on all afternoon via their link. She'd been telling him, too, the kind of things that his client, Mr. Duncan, had been spending the money on. Sable sat down but didn't say a word to either of them. Not then.

"Mr. Duncan, you've used most of the money we invested in your company to purchase personal items for yourself and your family." He simply waved him off, saying that with all the hard work they'd been doing, they deserved a nicer home, a better car and a long extended vacation. "No, not with my money, you shouldn't. That money was set to go for improvements on the lines you said were falling down around your ears. The new furnace and air conditioner to make it a better place to work for your employees. So far, nothing that you've used the money on has been used for any of the dozen or so things on the list that it was set up to use it on."

"You're not seeing the bigger picture here, Mr.

Griffin. Can I call you Garfield?" He told him no. If he'd not been looking right at the man, he might well have missed the anger that was there but only for a second. "The bigger picture is to make me feel like I'm heading toward something. The new items that I got with the money it's really helped me to think things through. Saved my marriage and family, too, I must admit. Now that everything in my personal life is right on schedule, I need to get down to business. And I can only do that if you give me another fifty grand."

"You said ten earlier. What have you thought of now that you need?" The man said that with the holidays coming up, he didn't want to shortchange his kids and wife after getting them all the other things. Garfield glanced at Sable when she stood up and handed both him and Mr. Duncan a file. "This is my wife, Sable. She's part of the firm that my family owns and operates. Go ahead, honey, tell him what you have found out."

"Thanks, Babe. I love you." Then she turned to Mr. Duncan. Her entire demeanor changed in that second. "You were given two hundred thousand dollars less than seven months ago. In that time, you've spent all of the money but for twenty grand on your new lifestyle. Not only have you purchased and paid cash for five new cars but three homes in other countries, beachfront property on both ends of the United States. As well as, you've put money in the Islands so that when you want to take off with more of the Griffin money, you'll be able to skip town in style."

"What do you think you're saying." Duncan looked at him. Now he could see the anger and fear on his face. "You don't believe her, do you? I mean, really? Why would I take advantage of you when you've been so generous with helping us out? I wouldn't. This is all a fabrication from her. Let me see your proof."

Sable opened up the file that she'd given him, and he saw where there was a great deal of the money that had been invested in Duncan had gone. Not only were there homes and cars, but it looked to him like Duncan had really put money in an account offshore. He laughed out loud when he saw that the accounts had been closed. Garfield would bet too that if he asked, all the property had been put on the market too.

"This means nothing. My wife did this. I had no idea." Duncan shoved the paperwork from Sable toward him. "I'll have a talk with her, and I'll find out what is going on. But we're still in business, right—" Duncan finally saw the zero balance on his accounts. "Where has that money gone. There was well over a hundred grand in this account. What have you done?"

"How would you know how much is in the account if your wife was the one that did it?" Duncan sputtered around while Sable continued. "The money has been put into another account until such time that we can verify that it belongs to the Griffin Foundation. All the properties have been put on the market too. Once they are sold, that money too will go into the account while someone, a neutral party, goes over your accounts to see where you were able to afford such large purchases."

"I had my parents die. That's where the money came from." Two death certificates were set in front of Duncan that claimed his mother and father died when he was nine. Also, there was paperwork from the attorney at that time that stated there was zero estate from his parents after they passed. "They might have found the money. You don't know that."

"I do, actually. I know a great deal more than you

do about this money. Like, for instance, the little bit of money that you paid your attorney to forge paperwork so that when your wife is murdered, I'm not saying you were going to do the murdering, but you are to get double the two million that you took out as a policy. Mr. Winehammer, your ex-attorney, has confessed that he was also to set up your wife being killed, along with your three oldest children, in a horrific cruise accident. You wanted him to make sure that a lot of people died so that it wouldn't come back on you." She tisked at him. "He said you were going to blame it on him if it came back on him that there weren't enough people killed. My goodness, you should have seen the look on your wife's face when I told her."

"You told her? Why would you do something like that? My goodness, you are causing me a great deal of heartache." He looked over at him and smiled. "You have to help me out of this mess, Garfield."

"I don't have to do shit. And it's Mr. Griffin to you." Garfield stood up when the police came into the room. Not just police but all kinds of agencies that had names on their vests. "It looks to me like you're going to be taken care of anyway. And once it's proven on what your plans are, I'm sure that my firm won't be out all that much. Especially after we take your home as well."

Duncan was still screaming about how this was none of his fault that he'd been framed. However, after looking over the paperwork that Sable had given them, he could see that Duncan had used not just his own social security number, but he also used a burner phone that Sable was able to unearth as well. He was mated to one smart cookie.

"It was with the help of all the women that I was able to find out this much so quickly. I heard that you were having a meeting with him, and I wanted to help. There is more, too, but this was enough to get him arrested. You don't mind, do you?" He pulled her onto his lap and held her. "I'm assuming that's a no, you don't mind."

"Nope. I don't mind at all when I don't have to spend the day with a man that planned to get his wife murdered. For that matter, I was just trying to figure out a way to get out of the meeting with him when I realized that I was not in a good enough mood to talk to him. He's been taking advantage of my good humor for far too long." Sable asked him what his plan was for the rest of the day. "Well, if I'm being honest with you, I'd like nothing more than to take you home and ravish you. But that would be entirely up to you."

"And what if I told you that I can't think of anything better than that very thing." Garfield tried not to get his hopes too far up, but when she turned in the seat he was in and faced him, he felt his cock stretch and his body respond hard to her scent. "I can feel your cock, Garfield. You're so hard. Do you have any idea how many nights I've gone to sleep so frustrated that I wanted to hunt you down and figure out why we've been putting this off for so long. What do you think?"

"I think that if you're teasing me, I'm going to die from blood loss." They both laughed, not diminishing the need one bit. In fact, he thought that he was needier than he'd been before. "I'm going to lay you out on my desk and taste the delights of you until I can't stand it anymore. Then I'm going to fuck you right here until neither of us can move."

Running his hand up her thighs to her bottom after stripping her of her clothing, he slid his hands under her until he was to her ribs. Up and over them, he did that several times as he fondled with her nipples when he got to them. He loved listening to her sounds when she was excited. Moans and small gasps of breath were making him feel like he was king of the world.

Standing up, he took one of her nipples into his mouth and nibbled on the hard tip. Even as she moved beneath him, moving her body upwards toward his cock, Garfield was careful not to let her get too close to him. If she did, if he entered her now, he'd come. While he was sure he could take her again, he wanted her to come with him the first time they were together.

As he'd teased her about as much as he could without taking her, he sat down in his chair and buried his mouth over her wet heat. Christ, he thought as she flooded his mouth with her creamy come. He thought that he could and would gladly spend the rest of his days sitting right here and having this for his meals.

Using his fingers, his tongue as well as his mouth, he tasted each and every time she came. The taste of her was rich in sweetness. Everything about her, every part of her, was more than he could have hoped for in a mate. Even as he took her over the edge again and again, he continued to feast on her pussy and cream as much as he could.

"Please. Garfield. I need you." He continued to eat her as she begged him to stop, to fill her. "If you don't stop and take me soon, I'm going to perish right here."

Standing up, his body stiff with need. His cock was covered in his thick cream. Garfield stood over her, fisting his cock while watching her cup her breasts with one hand and slide her fingers into her pussy with the other. If he didn't take her soon, like right now, he was going to come all over her, and that wasn't what he wanted.

He didn't so much as slide into her as he slammed forward. That was all it took for them both to cry out their releases. It wasn't enough, not nearly so. Garfield leaned over her to pull her up from the desk to his body and sat back down. For as much as he wanted to lay her out on the bed or floor, he knew this would be something that they'd both enjoy right now.

"Yes, fuck me." He didn't have to move. She was doing all the work riding him. When she hand-fed him her breasts, he took them in turn, suckling them and nibbling on each peak until she cried out her releases.

The tiny releases weren't what he wanted for either of them. But he was giving her as much as he could while still fucking her.

When her body bowed back, her eyes darkened with her coming. Garfield couldn't help but watch her as she seemed to be gathering up her release within her body. Every part of her seemed to come alive then. Her hair danced around her head, and bright sparks of light danced over her and around them. When she finally came, screaming out her release, Garfield watched her in wonder. She was the most beautiful creature, bar none. Then his own release took him.

Garfield didn't come, not like he had with other women. It was as if his body joined hers. And not in a sexual way, either. It was as if he became. What? He had no idea, but his body seemed to be twisting up and evolving. Again, he didn't know what into, but he knew that on every level of his life, he wasn't going to be the same man nor wolf again.

~*~

Sable didn't want to move ever again. Just getting the two of them to the bed had cost them both a great deal of energy and pain. Rolling to her side to look to see if Garfield was awake yet, he smiled at her.

"While I enjoyed that very much. However, I think that if we were to have sex like that again, I'd be incapacitated for the rest of my long life. Christ, what was that?" She grinned at him. "You have the energy to smile? Well, that's more than I have right now. Why don't you go down and get us some snacks? I'm famished but not willing to try the stairs."

Waving her hand over the blanket between them, a platter of meats and cheeses as well as fruit appeared between them. There were bottles of water and juice. Sitting up a little more, she took some of the dark grapes and ate two while opening a bottle of grape juice.

"I have a handle on the magic that we both share. It's been, I guess you could call it, downloaded into my mind so that I can use it. Did you get that too?" Garfield nodded that he had as he filled his mouth with some of the spicier meats that she'd made for them. "Also, I have a feeling that now that we've bonded, we'll be able to do things that we might not have before with the magic. Is this all right with you?"

"Yes. I mean, it could have come to us a little

nicer, but I'm not unhappy with the amount that we have. My wolf, he's a little pissy about it. I think that he was hurt a little while the transfer was taking place. Also, this is really strange, but I can feel him better than I had been able to before." She told him how she could also feel him. "You know, I think I knew that too. Like he's as much a part of you as he is me. That's odd."

They talked about all the things that they had discovered. The longer they lay there, enjoying the platter, the better she felt. Garfield said he felt better as well but wasn't up for another round of that kind of sex right way. She wasn't either, not yet, at any rate.

They both dozed off and on. When the sun was coming up, she got out of bed and took a long hot shower. Feeling better now that she had used the hot water to soothe out her muscles, she made her way downstairs after kissing Garfield and covering him up.

Sable decided to go and see what she could find out about Peter. She didn't want to think of him as her brother any more than she thought of Belinda as her sister. They were just two people that had the same bloodline as her, and that was all. They'd not been a part of her life, and she thought perhaps she might well like to keep it that way.

The hospital wasn't all that busy when she arrived. It only took her a few minutes to find out the floor and room that Peter was in. Going up to his room, she wasn't surprised to hear shouting coming from his room, nor a nurse coming out looking pissed off. Before the door to his room could come to a complete close, she slipped into it and stared at the mess that had been made on the wall across from her.

"What the fuck do you want?" She looked over at the man speaking to her. Christ, he looked older than her by decades. "Are you stupid? I asked you what the hell do you want?"

"I'm supposed to be your sister. Sable Parker Griffin." He stared at her for so long that she nearly asked him what the fuck he wanted. Instead, she made her way to the other side of the room where it looked as if he'd tossed his breakfast lunch and last night's dinner to it. "This is no way to get anything you want. Making a mess for others to clean up. Why would you do something like this?"

"Not that it matters to you, but I want you to get your ass busy and fix me. I can feel your magic now that I know to seek it out. It's strong enough to do what I tell you. Then you're going to give it to me. I'm not fucking around here. I should have gotten it because I'm older than you. Not to mention the male heir." Sable changed out the chair for something more comfortable for her, just to show off before sitting down. "I suppose you think you're going to make me beg. I'm not. You'll do as your told and be quick about it."

"You're very demanding for someone that is paralyzed from the waist down. I mean, you don't have enough magic to even toss me out of the room, correct?" He growled. "Yes, because that's a very grown-up thing to do. However, you should know that I have no intentions of *fixing* you, whatever that might entail. You've made yourself into what you are, and now it looks to me like you're going to have to live with it. I will say that you're making your life no better by being what you are right now. Or is that your normal way of dealing with things?"

"You will fix it so that I can walk again." She didn't even bother answering him. Even if it had been a question. "Did you hear me? I'm not going to be confined like this for the rest of my life."

"Now that I can help you with." He crossed his arms over his chest like he'd won a great battle with her. "I can end your life right now if that was an option you were giving me."

"No. Christ, you're worse than speaking to my mother." She pointed out that she'd been her mother as well. "No. I'm the one that says who she was mother to or not. And since I'm older than you, I say that you do not exist. Now, fix me."

Sable smirked at the blowhard ranting nonsense in the bed. "But you just said that I don't exist. If what you're telling me is true, then as a nonperson or, I guess, as a nonbeing, I can't fix you." Sable was enjoying this entirely too much and said as much to him. "You really are fairly stupid, aren't you? I mean, do you ever think about what you're saying before you say it? Doubtful, I think."

"I want you to fix it so that I have all your magic then. That should satisfy your sense of having things done in the correct order. Don't you think? Just hand it over." He put out his hand like he thought that would be the way it worked. Sable just smiled at him. "What is the matter now? Did I not say it the way that will make you get up off your ass and —"

"I don't know you. Well, I don't know any of you. Tell me about yourself. I have a pretty good idea of what sort of person you are. Maybe that's enough for now about you. Tell me about our father. Or your father. Whatever you want to call him." He said that he was just a man. "An aging man, from what I've heard. All the magic that was for him to use when mother was around is leaving him. I'm not sure how that works either, but that's what I was told. Belinda came to visit me. Did I mention that before?"

"No, you didn't. And don't believe a word she tells you. She's been out to get me since the day I was born." Sable told him that she thought that they were both deserving of each other. "I don't know what that means, but if you're telling me that we're alike, I guess you could say that's true. Belinda and I did have our fun together. She was forever good at plotting things that we'd do. Adventures, she called them. Anyway, she's the reason that I'm injured the way that I am. If she'd just left her door closed instead of coming out when she had, then nothing would have happened to me."

"What sort of plotting did the two of you do? The reason I'm curious about that is that I was raised as an only child. I never went on adventures of any kind. Well, not any that would involve me getting into trouble. I bet the two of you were in trouble a great deal." He laughed manically, and it made the hairs on her arms dance. "What sort of things did the two of you do?"

"It was against our Aunt Grace that we had the most fun with. Because we were related to her, she couldn't harm us. Not even when we hurt her. She was stronger, so she had to just walk away. She hated us. With good reason, I guess. We would harass the little people and hurt them, too, I guess. Is this your plan? To take up where we stopped?

"Grace can be such a stickler for things too. She didn't want us to bother the new flowers. We weren't to knock the new blooms around where they'd drop the newborns. That's how faeries are made, did you know that? They're born in blooms. Oh, and we weren't allowed to pull their wings off them. We did make quite a few of them suffer too." He looked like the memory of what he'd done was making him nostalgic for past deeds. He had a wistful smile. It made her positively ill to think of what the two of them had been up to. "Ah, the memories. Thanks for bringing them up. But as for our father? Well, I guess you could call him nothingness. He wasn't abusive, mores the pity. Nor did he take part in the punishments that mother gave us. Usually, he could be counted on to get us out of them. But he really wasn't all that much of anything, really."

"Where is he now? I know that Belinda told me that he was fading away. But I thought that I'd go see him." Peter told her she wasn't going anywhere until she handed over the magic. Sable smirked again at his arrogance. "Yes, well, we'll see about that, won't we."

Disappearing from the room, the first time she'd done anything like that, Sable took herself to the room that she shared with Garfield. He was still there but showering. Joining him in the warm spray wasn't enough, and she scrubbed at her skin with a loofah hard enough that he pulled it away from her. Crying, telling him everything that had happened since she left him, he carried her out of the bathroom with a towel around her and held her on the bed until she was calmer.

"It sounds like you were right not to trust Belinda." She told Garfield that she didn't trust any of them. "Yes, I can see that. But as I've said before, we know Lady Grace. Perhaps if you were to go and talk to her, you'd get a less creepy side of the story. Maybe not. She might well tell you all they did simply because she might be frustrated with them. I know I would have been hard-pressed not to have murdered them in their beds."

"I'll do that. But not right now." He asked her what she wanted to do. "I don't know. But I don't want to think of family anymore. Not mine, at least. Let's do something without considering the cost or how long it takes. Even out to dinner someplace very fancy."

"I think I can arrange that." He continued to hold her as he rocked back and forth. "Sable, I love you very much."

"And I love you, Garfield. Very much so." And she did. If she never had to have contact with her family again, Sable thought that she could live with that. But she had a feeling that she was going to have to see them again. If for no other reason than to set some things straight. And her having the magic was going to be a problem for not just Peter, but Sable thought for Belinda too. The verdict was still out about her father. She was going to have to go and meet him soon, too, she knew.

Chapter 4

Garfield knocked on the door to the house he'd been sent to again. He didn't want to be here, but since Grace had asked him to run point on this one, he couldn't refuse her. As soon as he heard footsteps coming toward the door, he stepped to the side of the door and didn't stand directly in front of it. She had told him several times to be on his guard.

The door creaked open. Like one would see in a horror movie. The darkness beyond didn't help his level of fear either. It wasn't until the frail, he supposed very frail man stepped into the opening that he felt he had the wrong house.

"Yes? What is it?" He told him who he was. "I

don't know you. If you know me, that's well and good. I'm Patrick. If I had a last name, I no longer remember it. What is it you wish, young man? I'm very old and not getting any younger standing here waiting on you to decide if you're coming in or not."

"My name is Garfield Griffin. I'm a wolf shifter. An ancient. Never mind. That's not important right this minute. Were you the mate of someone by the name of Shirley? I don't remember if I had her last name either. And you'd have children by the names of Peter and Belinda." Patrick asked him what they'd done now. Then he said he wanted nothing to do with them. "Yes, I don't blame you there. I've not met them, but they've talked to my mate. May I come in?"

"I don't know what you'd want from me, but if you're insistent on coming in, you're going to have to make me a pot of tea. I've not had a good one in a few weeks. I keep burning the water." He wasn't entirely sure how one went about burning water, but he needed some answers, and if he had to make tea to get them, so be it. Patrick began walking away, and Garfield entered the house, closing the door behind him as he followed the other gentleman. "Belinda gives off this air that she's so helpful and nice. I wouldn't trust her in a rattlesnake cage without having them all killed off. And that son Peter. He'd be able to pass off as a snake himself. They're both not worth the spit it took to make them. The tea is in the cupboard there. And my cup is in the sink. I think that it's still in one piece. When she was here the other day, she did nothing but bang things around and—" Patrick looked up at him with one eye. "You're the mate to my daughter. Sable. Something. Griffin, like you said. Yes, I've heard about her. She's gotten all the magic. Good for her. I'm sure she's no better than the other two."

"You'd be surprised. She's smart. Works a full-time job. And the magic isn't really that important to her. Would you like to meet her?" He just eyed him, and Garfield just laughed. "All right then. I'll make you some tea."

As he went through the process of making a stout cup of tea as Patrick wanted, he told him about what he'd been up to today. It was just filling out the silences, but Patrick did ask questions of him. When he set the cup in front of him, giving him a choice of lemon and milk, Garfield sat down with his own tea.

"My wife, she's gone. I'm not entirely sure what happened. Really I don't care. But she's gone, and I've been all alone for the last few days. Well, more if you want the truth of it. She and I didn't hang out like people do, I guess. She had her things. I had mine. I'm supposing that she finally found the one, the other daughter and gave her the magic. She'd been telling me that same story for years. Never believed her. But then, I was forced into this sham of a life, and I didn't pay much attention to anything going on around me. When did she have this daughter of mine?" Garfield said Sable had been a twin of Peters. "Could have been. I wasn't there for that birth. I don't remember rightly what it was that kept me away, but…I think I was in trouble about one thing or another. I was in a prison cell if I remember. Something about some missing books. Whatever they were, they must have turned up not too long after Peter was born. I can see her doing that to me. Keeping me away. Why? You might as well ask that floor over there why she did most of the things that she did. Wouldn't get you answered any other way. Grace. She might know. Now there was a fine woman. I was set to be her husband when all this came up about Shirley carrying my child. Don't know how the other one, well, two happened either. Not any of them are my children. I've never slept with Shirley. Not once. I had a dream once. That Grace and I were... well, that's personal. But I didn't sire those kids. So how she had them? Well, I guess she had her ways too."

"I'm sorry to hear that, sir. I am." He waved him off, sipping his tea. "How is it? My mom loves a nice hot cup of tea. She taught all of us how to make one so that if we married, we'd know one thing that a wife would like. My wife, she doesn't care for hot tea." Patrick laughed.

"Neither did Shirley. But me? Well, I tell you, son, you can make me a cup anytime you want. This is wonderful." Patrick told him where the cookie tin was, and he was able to unearth it from a dark cabinet for them both. "When I was a young man, there were all kinds of things going on in the world I'm from. Not from here, mind you, but where Grace lives. I was a man of worth, you see but not good enough for my Grace."

"I'm sorry to hear about that. I don't believe in things like that. Where you can't marry because of some kind of sect or because of money." He said he noticed that no one feels that way nowadays, either. "So how did you end up with Shirley over Grace, if you don't mind me asking."

"Grace is the queen of the earth. I'm sure you know that if you know her. I can smell her scent on you. It's not very strong, but it's there. Anyway, she was being trained, and I was with her. Then one day, I ended up being told, just told, that I was to marry Shirley because she was with child. My child. That was decades ago. I knew from the start that it wasn't going to work out with us. But we did get along better than most. Like I said, she had her ways, and I had mine. Then after Belinda was born, things sort of continued like we were friends of a sort. I never had anything to do with Belinda. I guess you could say that I didn't want to love another man's child. I shouldn't have done that. I know that now. It wasn't her fault. And in doing what I did, I lost out on knowing her. Then when Peter came along. And I guess Sable, I just distanced myself from him too. Didn't like him much from the first time I saw him. He had a look about him that made me think he'd stab me in the back, even as little as he was. I think

Shirley felt the same way when she handed him off to nannies and the like and didn't bother with him."

"I'm to understand that he has sold off information about Sable to some people that wish to find her and tear her apart to see what she's made of." Patrick said that that sounded like him. Belinda too. "They sound like a pair."

"You've no idea. I mean, just because I've not had much to do with them, I have kept tabs on them. I didn't want to be blindsided by anything that they did. It wasn't until a few years ago that I found out that I had another daughter. Or a child was born of this marriage, I guess. But, too, I had nothing to do with that one either." Garfield said that she was very different from her sister and brother. "She couldn't be much worse than them, I guess. I know that was mean and uncalled for, but you have no idea what the two of them here have been doing over the years. Or, perhaps you do. You said you were an ancient."

"I am. And you'd be right. I have seen and heard things that would make a human sad for their race." Nodding, the two of them enjoyed the last of their tea. Asking Patrick if he'd like to have dinner with him and Sable tonight, he declined. "It wouldn't be any trouble for us to take you there and bring you back if that is the issue for you. I've enjoyed our talks and the information that you've imparted to me."

"You should ask that wife of yours. She might have it in her head that we're not any of us to be trusted. For all you know, I could be the most horrible person in the world and just biding my time until I can get the two of you alone to sell you off." Storm appeared in the room suddenly. She put her fingers to her lips and shook her head. Garfield felt his wolf run along his skin when someone knocked on the front door. "That would be Belinda. She was coming here to talk to me about a few things. You stay there, no matter what she might say to either of us." When Patrick got up to go let her in, Sable appeared with Storm. Storm told him what was going on.

"He can't see nor hear us. But I'd like for you to tell him that Belinda is in trouble with the law. She thinks she can hide out here and then blame Patrick for what she's done." He asked her what it was she'd done. "She is being questioned about the *accident* that Peter had. She tripped him when he fell. Then while he was out, she hit him in the back with a bat, and that is why he's paralyzed. These are some nice people."

When Patrick returned to the kitchen with Belinda, he could tell they'd been arguing. Over what, he didn't know, but he was going to protect the other man if it came to it. Asking Patrick again if he'd like to have dinner with him tonight, the man seemed to be confused for a second.

"I've spoken to my wife, and she's all for it. She's had a long day herself and wants to get out around town for a while." Patrick said he thought he'd enjoy that. Both of them, he noticed, were careful not to mention his wife's name. "Great. If you're ready, we can go now."

"Gee, thanks, I'd love to go too. Thanks for being so polite in asking me." Garfield told Belinda she wasn't invited. "Well, aren't you just rude? Father isn't going to go either. He and I have things to discuss, and since you're being such a dick about things, you'll just have to have dinner all by your lonesome."

"I don't know if you're aware of this or not, Belinda, but I'm an adult who makes his own decision. Same as you. If you have things to discuss with me, spill it. I've got a date tonight, and I'm not going to be dilly-dallying around here with you." Belinda stared at her father for several seconds, and he let her. "Well? What is it you wanted to talk about?"

"You're different. Something…I don't know what it is, but you're different than you were. Did you dye your hair?" Garfield looked at Patrick then. He was different. "What have you been up to?" While they argued about what Patrick had supposedly done, Sable spoke to him.

"It's you, Garfield. You've given him hope. Also, magic to keep him safe." Sable smiled at him, and Garfield felt like he could take on the world. "You couldn't do that unless he was deserving of it. I didn't notice it because I've not seen him before now. The only one in the family to trust is a man that was tricked into everything."

Standing up, he was happy to see that Belinda backed up. Letting just a little of his wolf show, he asked Patrick if he was ready. As soon as he turned his back on Belinda, she reached out to grab the other man. Luckily he had been watching, or he might well have been seriously hurt. As it was, he was only just able to shift and let the weight of his wolf take them both to the floor, with the knife sticking him deeply in his chest. He lay there for several seconds, waiting for his blood to bleed out of him. But it didn't happen. Once the pain subsided, it felt as if nothing at all had happened.

Biting her wrist, she cried out in pain and then dropped the knife. Patrick kicked it away and then sat down in the closest chair. Thankfully it was far enough away from Belinda that he felt better for the man. Both Storm and Sable disappeared, and he was slightly worried about that. But when there was another knock at the front door, he asked Patrick twice if he'd go and answer it. When he returned, he was with the police. Telling them about how Belinda had tried to murder him.

"I see there has been some fun around here that I missed. I was told that you'd be here holding onto my prisoner. You're Garfield, correct?" Without releasing Belinda, he nodded at the officer. He didn't know who he was as yet as he was behind him. "Thanks for the help. Belinda Smith, we're here to talk to you about your involvement in the accident with your brother. He is now claiming that you hit him." Belinda screamed, telling someone to get the fucking dog off her. Then she said that her father had done it. He hated Peter. Garfield wondered if Sable or one of the other women had something to do with his sudden remembering of her hitting him. "Well, that's not the way it sounds to me. Since you just tried to kill both of them. How about we take this downtown and have a talk about it."

"I'm not going anywhere with you. I want you to get this animal off me before I get pissy." No one moved or asked him to move, so he didn't. Garfield liked knowing that she couldn't harm anyone else today. "You fucking idiots. Does no one see that this thing is hurting me? He just attacked me for no reason whatsoever. Get it off of me."

Once it was established that he would hold her until cuffs were put on her, Garfield slowly got off of Belinda. The knife was still sticking in his chest, but there was no blood surrounding the area. It made him slightly ill to see it sticking in his body. Wondering how he'd get it out of him before he was able to shift, he was startled when Sable showed up in the back yard where he went to change.

Without saying a word to him, she wrapped her hand around the pummel of it and pulled it out of him quickly. It hurt worse coming out than it had going it. Still, there was no blood. Shifting and dressing while still on the ground, he looked up at Sable when she said his name.

"You're fine. You know that, don't you?" He nodded, still dealing with the sting of the knife coming out of him. He rubbed the sore spot on his chest. "We didn't know if you could shift with it being stuck in you, so your mom sent me here to help you. But I couldn't stand seeing it in you still. I'm sorry if I hurt you."

"You didn't. Not really. I think it was more of a shock than anything else. Are you all right?" She nodded and sat down on the ground too. "Belinda was going to kill him. I had to act fast. I like Patrick."

"I do as well. I've been doing some thinking about things. I'm not ready to share yet, I might well be wrong, but I'm thinking that I'm not going to be. The police are charging her with the attempted murder of you and Patrick." He said he didn't want to talk about Belinda right now. She laughed, which was what he'd been going for. "I love you, you big dope. Very much."

"I love you too. I'd better get back in there and see if they need anything from me. Are you really all right?" Nodding, she stood up and told him she was going to see Peter again. "All right. I'll see you later then."

He was glad to see that Belinda had already been taken away. The officer first on the scene asked him if he would fill out a statement, leaving out that he'd had to shift. After being handed a pad of paper and a pen, Garfield set to work. Christ, all he'd done was come to see about Patrick. And perhaps have some dinner with him. But this was one less person that he had to worry about in Belinda coming around.

All Garfield did was write down what had come natural to him. He wrote out a detailed report of what had happened and what was said. And, as asked, he left out the part where he'd had to take her down as his big wolf.

~*~

Peter wasn't happy. But he was having a bit of fun. He couldn't get in touch with his sister. Either of them, for that matter. They had to fix him. Damn it, it was humiliating not being a real man when he was stuck in the bed like he was. Laying his head back so he could think, the sound of laughter had him looking at the chair he'd ordered to have put in here.

No reason for it to be in his room, really. But it was one of the few things he had some control over. Sable was sitting there looking at him when he saw it was her. In his chair.

"If you're not here to fix me, then go away. I've had enough shit happen today that I don't have the stomach to talk to anyone." She said that she'd heard that he was being trained on how to clean himself up. "Yes. Nasty too. I've decided that I'm not eating again. I know that it's not going to happen, but for now, I'm never eating again. What do you want?"

"I have a few questions for you. If you answer them, I'll tell you something you might be able to use. Tit for tat, you might call it." He said that he didn't want to talk about tits anymore. "I'm sure you understand that isn't what I was talking about."

"I know. I'm in a sour mood, thanks to Belinda. Where is she, anyway? I've been trying to reach her all damned day." Sable said that she was in jail. For the attempted murder of Patrick. That news did surprise him. "Really? Christ, I knew she was stupid. Why would she kill off the hand that feeds her? I don't think she—wait. How did she kill him? I mean, isn't there a rule or something about that?"

"There is. I told you that she was arrested for the attempted murder. I've been thinking about a lot of things along those lines. But me first on my question. Why did you tell Shirley that you wanted to kill off all the women in the world.?"

Peter frowned and shook his head. "I didn't. I said it, but it was to Grace. Not my mother. She was never around when I needed her." She asked him if he was sure. "I know the difference between my mother and my aunt. I was like ten years old and had just had my heart ripped out by some girl in my class." He shrugged. "I don't even remember her—Bethann Davies. Anyway, I didn't have any idea what I was talking about. But I said it to Grace. Not my mother. Why?"

"Is that your question to me?" He shook his head. Why did he care why she was curious about him being ten? "All right. You can ask me a question, or I can tell you something you don't know about the magic you hold."

"Magic. Without a doubt, I will always pick magic." She told him what she knew. "No. You're wrong about that. I tried to fix myself, and it didn't work. I exhausted myself trying to get it to work. Nothing. You have to tell me something that is true, don't you? I mean, I didn't lie to you."

"No, you didn't. And I didn't either. You do have the ability to heal yourself. I didn't say magic. I said ability." He asked her what the difference was. "Magic means that you have the power to heal yourself. The ability means that you have the means to fix yourself if you really want it."

"I don't understand." She nodded at him as if he was stupid or something. He found this sister more irritating than Belinda. His temper flared again. "This isn't working. I'm done with you."

"There is a nurse bringing you in your dinner. I want you to be polite to him." He asked her why he should do that. All the nurses here were idiots. Sable tisked at him. "I'm helping you to understand the difference in ability. Just be polite to him the entire time that he's here. You can do that. This one time."

Mark, a very large nurse, brought him in his tray. Before it was put on the table in front of him, he was asked if he was going to be any trouble today. Just for a split second, he wanted to lash out. Looking at Sable, he decided that he'd give it a try.

"I'm sorry." Mark stood still, staring at him. "I am. I won't give you any trouble. I swear. I've had a terrible week. As you might know. I am sorry."

"Well, all right then." After his tray was sat on the table, Mark took away the trash from the crackers he'd had earlier. He felt set. "Would you like some fresh water? I can get you a couple of glasses of ice with some water if you want it."

"Yes. I'd like that." When he turned and left him, Peter looked at Sable. "What did that prove? Nothing. You're just trying to make me look stupid. And he'll be twice as pissed when I turn into myself again."

"Wiggle your toes." He glared at her. Telling her, she wasn't the least bit funny. "I'm not trying to be. When you use your ability to heal yourself, being nice, it will heal your body too."

He did what she asked. While he didn't expect

anything to happen, he watched as the little toe on his left foot did indeed move. Not taking his eyes off of what was happening, he asked when the rest of his body would be healed.

"This is an ability, Peter. Not magic. You have to change yourself in order for the changes to happen to your body. It won't be a huge change all at once, but little changes like your toe. It's entirely up to you to be able to make it so that you can walk again." His water was brought in, and he was too excited to be anything but nice to Mark again.

"I got you a soda too. I know you were asking for one, so I got it for you. You need to sip it. If you don't, then you're going to be sick, and that won't be good for you." Thanking him, not even thinking about it, Peter told him too that he'd be careful about drinking it. "You're welcome. Thanks, Peter."

After Mark left, he wiggled his toe a little bit more. Looking at Sable, he asked her what was going to happen now. Was this all he was going to get?

"That's entirely up to you. However, there are consequences to your progress if you fail to work on yourself." He asked her what she meant. "If you were to turn back into your old self, you'll lose all the progress that you have acquired now. Say if you're entire leg is mobile. Then you say something nasty or do something to someone for the pure joy of it for yourself, you'll have to start over. All the progress that you have will simply disappear."

"Well, that sucks. What if someone is mean to me, and I retaliate? That doesn't seem fair to me." She told him that it was something that he was going to have to think about rather than just lashing out at people. "This isn't going to be an overnight fix. This is going to take time, I'm thinking."

"Yes. But I think you can do it. You've already made some lead way into getting your toe to work. I don't know how long it will take you to be walking again, but I can see you being able to get it working for you." He nodded, processing what she'd just told him. "Peter, it's my turn to ask a question. What can you tell me about Belinda? I don't want her to get out of jail if she's done something terrible that needs to be addressed. I know that she's been around longer than either of us. I was wondering if she had told you anything."

"You want me to rat on my sister." He wasn't angry by it but was making sure that was what she wanted him to do. When she nodded, Peter laid his head back on the bed and thought about all the things that Belinda had told him she'd done. Even as recently as a month ago. But did he want to tell on her? His toe wiggled, and he knew that if he was going to make this happen for himself, not selfishly but to get back on his feet, so to speak, he was going to have to make sacrifices of himself to get there. Maybe this would be a good start. "She told me that she had some trouble with one of the men that worked for her. He wasn't playing ball or something along those lines." He looked at Sable and shook his head. "I'm not saying I'm one hundred percent sure she isn't lying to me, but she did tell me this. The man is in a well that is on the property that we live on. She told me…if you have a weak stomach, I'd have someone else go there. She said that she taught them all a lesson in what it means to cross her. He's…she told me that she mutilated him. While I'm not sure what that would entail, but she is a sadist, and I've seen her work before."

"Thank you for that. I know that it must be hard

on you for telling on her. But if she were to be released from jail right now, I have a feeling that she'd try and hurt you again. This time it might be something that no amount of magic or goodwill will be able to cure." He nodded but felt his heart hurt for the things that Belinda might do to Sable as well. He told her to be careful. "I will. And thank you for that, Peter. When they're ready to put you into a facility to help you cope with being injured, Garfield and I will make sure that you have the best of care. Not because of this, but because you were kind to me today." When she stood up, he found he didn't want her to leave him. He had misjudged her. "I'll be back. Soon. And I'm going to make sure that you have everything you need while in here. You'll get better, Peter, I know it. But I will be back so often that you'll beg me to stop coming."

"I don't think so." He thought about all the things he missed in the two of them not being together. "I wish I might have—no, that's not true. If we had been together, I don't know what I might have done to you. You were better off not being around me or Belinda. You're a good person."

"So are you." She leaned over and kissed him on

the forehead. Peter felt his eyes fill with tears. When she wiped them off his cheek, she kissed him there. "I'll be back. If you need anything, just let me know. You can contact me through a link that we share. Just think of talking to me, and you'll be able to. I'm happy that we're together now, Peter. So very happy."

When she left him, he lay there and sobbed for all the things that he had missed because she'd been taken away. It was good, a very good thing that she had, but he did have to wonder if he might well have been a better person if he had her around. More than likely not, but the choice had been taken from him. Again, he thought it was a good thing too.

Wiggling his toe, he noticed that he could now move three of them. Peter was so giddy with happiness that he decided that he was going to remember everything that Belinda had told him and write it down. If this is what being a good person was all about, he was going to stick to it. Yes, he thought to himself as he sipped his soda. He was going to be a better person and the kind of person that Sable could be proud to call her brother.

Eating his now cold dinner wasn't bad. He was

told, too, that he needed to make sure that he ate as much as he could because it would add to his strength. While he had no idea how that worked, he was going to keep doing what he was told by the professionals in order to be healthy when he was able to walk and get around again. Peter even enjoyed the rest of his soda without gulping it down as he might have done before because he'd been told not to.

When his tray was taken away, Peter made sure that he thanked the nurse. He also asked her if he could have a pen and paper. He needed to make notes. As soon as he was alone again, he turned on the television and watched a movie he'd never seen before. Peter thought that he could get used to being this kind of person. It sure was easier on his head when he wasn't pissed off all the time. Laughing a little, he thought of all the things he was going to tell Sable about.

Chapter 5

Jeffery looked over the specs he'd been given to set up the dish he was installing on one of the downtown buildings the family owned. They were planning to use the building as a centralized location for Garfield and Sable to work from, and he'd been asked to make sure they had a good, secure network. Honestly, he'd rather be having his nails clipped as his wolf than to work on something so mundane as a dish network.

"You know that you can just do that with the magic that you have." He nearly fell backward off the building when Storm appeared before him. He growled at her and told her to be careful next time. "I'm sorry. You were feeling so sorry for yourself that I could have knocked you off anyway, and you'd not noticed. Why are you bothering with the actual work of this when all you need to do is just make it work magically. It would more than likely be more secure too."

"I guess I never thought about it." He sat back on his butt and looked at Storm. "I have a couple of questions for you. You don't have to tell me if it's some kind of rule you can't break but do I have a mate out there too? The reason that I ask is, I don't—"

"Yes, you all have mates. And if you were going to tell me that you don't want one, then tough shit. She's coming, and you'll love her." He laughed. "That's not what you were going to say, is it? I've been off the handle all day. I need a distraction so I can think about the issue that I'm having with someone in town stealing. So what was it you were going to say you didn't want?"

"I don't want to be not ready. I know I have a home that is, for the most part, not furnished. I never saw a need for it before as I spend most of my time working. Also, it's a big flipping house, in the event you didn't know, and it would take me a while to get my shit together and fill it." She asked him why he didn't just fill it with things he found. "I don't really socialize all that much. My idea of a fun Saturday night is to order a pizza, watch something on television, then go to bed. As I said, not much of a socializer. I know that I could easily buy things that I want online. But that seems so cold to me. I was perhaps wondering if you or one of the other women could help me out with that."

"You mean to fill out your home for another woman that will more than likely want her own things? Sure, let us get right on that for you." He told her she didn't need to be nasty. "No. You're right. I didn't. Sorry. Maybe if I tell you my issue, you can help me. There is this guy that owns the grocery store in town that is claiming that he's being robbed once a week. Now, I'd not take much faith in his narrative except that he's claiming that some kid — I have no idea why he thinks it's a kid because he doesn't know who is robbing him — is coming around and stealing things like bandages, bread and peanut butter. Not bandages every week but once a month. The bread and peanut butter makes me believe that someone is homeless and that's all they need to eat. Protein and bread, I'm thinking."

"Sounds like either it's not a kid because I'm thinking a kid would be more into chips and candy than an adult. Or, and this one is what I'm leaning toward more now that I think about it, it's a child and an adult. Perhaps they are homeless or just very poor. Do you have someone around town that you think it is? Or do you know?" She said she didn't know as it was hard to see who it was. "All right. You don't know. So. It could be a kid but not a teenager. The reason that I say that is because, as a teenager, they'd stick out more. Who would notice a child stealing from you. Especially if the kid has had lots of practice."

"Why do you say that? I'm not saying that you're wrong, but why say they have practice? By the way, I've gotten into your head and fixed the internet and cable for this place. I think I'll do the same for all the houses. It's much safer not to mention something that we could all use with the amount of money this family has. Security has to be used over paying the cable company each month. Not that I won't go ahead and pay them, but this will be ours to keep all of us safe. But back to my question, why do you think they have practice?"

"Well, the store owner, his name is Bill Harman, by the way, Bill doesn't know who is taking the things. Nor do you. Practice makes perfect, and that's what I'm thinking. I have to admit, the bandage part gives me some pause. It indicates that someone needs them, as in they're hurt. I don't like that thought at all." She said she'd not even considered that. "You've been too focused on it for too long. Fresh eyes and all that. But, we have to find this person or persons before—Storm, do you know that this is one of our mates? Is that why you came to me? Christ. If that's the reason I'm going to stay home until you get—"

She laughed at him. "I swear to you that never entered my mind. Oh, you are so paranoid about shit. If she is your mate, if it is even a female, then you're going to love her and the child. I'd have a talk with him about stealing, but this is all for a good cause too. That will make me laugh for a month if she is one of your mates." He told her that he didn't like her overly much. "Yes, you do. You and the others all love me. I'm going to go into town and see what I can find out. Maybe I can trace them by touching the items that are being taken. Come with me. Your work here is finished, thanks to me. So come with me because you owe me."

"All right. I'm not happy with you right now, but you did help us all out." He was glad to be doing something that felt productive if he was honest with himself. Jeffery knew, too, that he needed to get out more. "Where are we going first? I was thinking that we should see how many empty buildings are around that might have someone in them. Also, it's September now. We need to locate this little family before it gets too cold."

"Yes, that was something that I was just thinking about too. They'd not have electricity, or they'd be getting things they could cook. Water too. But then I just remembered that all the buildings here are on city water and it's on no matter if there is power or not. But that would be cold regardless." He said she was thinking now and was happy for her. "Yes. As you said, I needed to have some help seeing what I wasn't before."

As they walked around town, they also picked up a few things they needed at home. Since he was helping her, Storm invited him to her home for dinner.

Meatball subs were on the menu, and he couldn't have been happier to say yes. He was taking the things they'd picked up and putting them into his car when he thought of which building it might be the family was using.

They started for there as he explained why he thought that was the house. "It's been abandoned for a few months now. I think the couple that lived there were in arrears for a great many house payments and just took off. It could be that if this family is living there, they're well situated in that they'd have all the comforts of home. I don't even think that the power has been turned off." They stood across the street from the house he was thinking about. "I wanted to buy this house when it came on the market. I think that the couple that did end up buying it was a young couple with a couple of kids. I backed off when I saw that. I wish now that I hadn't. Not that I couldn't have outbid them, but it seemed like the perfect home for a little family starting out."

He watched as a kid came out from behind the house. Storm said that she could make them shadows, and he'd never see them if they were to walk right up on them. As soon as they were in the yard, he smelled them. Whoever they were, the kid was a wolf. He told Sable that he had to notify Edwin about them being here.

"Not yet. I'll tell him but not yet. I have a feeling that whatever is going on with them, notifying a wolf would be death for them both." Nodding, he asked her if she knew that they were both males. "Yes. I felt that as soon as we got to the house. I guess you're off the hook for now."

The boy was rinsing out some clothing. He would have thought that there was a washer and dryer still in the home as he'd been told that nothing but a couple of pieces of luggage filled with clothing had been taken from the house. When the boy stared at where they were standing, Jeffery asked Storm to let him see them. The kid was calmer than he might have been if someone would have popped in front of him.

"My name is Jeffery Griffin. This is my sister-in-law, Storm Griffin. We're not going to harm you." He said that he didn't care if they did or not. "I'm sorry to hear that. We'd like to help you and whoever you're protecting in the house." He looked toward the house and then back at him.

"He's dying. I've tried to take care of him, but he refused to be seen by a doctor. He's not wolf like we are." Storm asked if he was related to him. "No. I mean, I think he wanted to be at one time, but since my mom was killed about six months ago, he's been — the new pack leader killed her because she wouldn't submit. Park was hurt in trying to protect her. He is bleeding out from the wounds."

Storm left them there to go into the house. "My brother is the pack alpha around here. I'm not sure what's going on with your pack or where you're from, but we'll have to let him know you're here. And about the other pack leader." The boy, who'd still not shared his name, said it wouldn't do any good. He just killed whoever went up against him. "We'll see about that."

A car pulled into the drive, and he wasn't the least bit surprised to see Edwin getting out of it. Not only was he there, but so was their dad. Edwin went into the house, and dad came to be with him and the boy.

"My name is Charlie Griffin. I have you some food in the car if you've got a mind to having it." The boy said he'd like that. "Good. You're not stupid. I can feel your hunger from here. I was fearful that you'd turn it down. It's in the back seat. Have you a seat there and enjoy it. Now, if you start with the cupcakes, I won't tell my missus. I'll just say I told you to go there, and that's what you did. What's your name, by the way?"

"Andrew Bailey. No one has ever called me anything but Drew, however." Dad told him that he'd do the same. "Thank you. I'll let you guys talk while I eat then."

When he walked away, dad turned to him. "He's starving. Did you feel that, son?" He told his dad that he had then told him what Drew had told him about the other pack. "Yes, I've heard of some leaders doing that. Never cottoned to it myself. Nasty business that. But Edwin will take care of him and the man. What do you know about Mr. Dresher?"

"The man? Nothing. Not even his name until now. Storm and I only just got here." He told him about the theft at the store, and they had deduced that it had to be someone homeless. "Good job on that. Good job. All right then. We'll see about getting them home with us. Your momma was cooking up a lot of food when she heard there was a young man that needed her. She's been feeling a mite down lately without having anything to do. I've been thinking on taking her on a vacation, but now that he's here, she'll be happy for a bit."

He didn't like that his mom was feeling like she hadn't anything to do. Jeffery decided that he was going to stop over to see her more often than he had been. Maybe she'd be a little nicer to him about helping him with his home. She might well tell him the same thing that Storm had, but she'd be a good deal nicer to him. Then maybe not. She'd been hanging around with the women of the family a great deal lately and had started acting like them. Jeffery laughed to himself. She'd be called a pepper if his grandda had anything to say about it.

Drew was finished eating by the time he and dad made it over to the car. He'd not started with the cupcakes. In fact, he'd not eaten either of them. Dad told Drew that he was smart for pacing himself. Not having a lot of food for a while could make you sick when you got it again. Dad would know. He'd been a starving man when mom had found him.

Edwin was coming out with Dresher when he and his dad were helping Drew clean up the yard. For being only ten, the kid seemed to have a good head on his shoulders. While they were working, he started up a conversation with him about his other pack as well as his mom. He was a little hesitant about talking about the other alpha, but he did talk about how wonderful his mom had been.

"She worked really hard for me to be able to go to a private school. I think she was trying even then to save me from the alpha. He had his eyes on her since he found out that my real father had been killed when I was five. When she wouldn't submit to him, he broke her neck and dared anyone to bury her. Allen and I moved her body so that he'd not know and then took off. We've been running from him since." Jeffery asked him if the alpha had found them. "A few times, yeah. He hurt Allen again. Telling him that he'd not heal until he forgave him. I'm not sure what he thought he needed to be forgiven for, but we take off every time we get wind of him coming around."

"He didn't get to kill you when he killed your mother. That was, from what it sounds like was going through his head, what he was thinking. Killing your mother was wrong, don't get me wrong. But once he did that, he knew that he had an enemy of you and didn't want you coming around to take him out when you were older." Drew nodded but didn't look like he was convinced. "Do you have plans of getting the alpha back for killing your mother?"

"I did. But I also know that I'm only a kid. I can keep telling myself that I'm going to grow up someday, but all I can think about is if he finds me, which he's looking really hard, he'll kill me off. Somedays, well, a lot of days, I wish he would. I'm just a kid, and I'm not sure how much more I can do this adulting thing. That's what my mom called it. Adulting. When you have to do things that are above what you think you're capable of doing." He looked away. "She would tell me all the time that revenge is something that will eat at your heart and soul if you allow it. I know that she was right in that. I feel wrung out most of the time."

Without thought as to what he was doing, he pulled the boy toward him and hugged him. It took Drew a few seconds to hug him back, but when he did, he sobbed on his chest for a good while as Jeffery held him. When his dad and brother came toward them, he shook his head. They both turned and left him to Drew. The kid was limp with pain when he finally pulled back.

"You must think I'm a baby." Jeffery shook his head and told him that he thought he was a man that had been given a lot and just needed a minute. "I'm only ten, not a man."

"You've been doing a man's job and doing it well for six months, Drew. Your age didn't even come into it when you saw a job that needed to be done and did it. Your mom would have been very proud of the way that you've not only kept yourself safe but Allen as well." Drew thanked him. "No need for that. I thank you for trusting that I'd not hurt you when you needed it most."

By the time they were at his parents' home, Drew was dozing off. The kid really had been through a great deal in the last half of year, and he didn't blame him at all for catching a nap when he needed it. Instead of taking him to the kitchen with the rest of the family was gathered, mom took Drew upstairs, telling him that he could take a shower and that she'd laid out some clothing for him to use. She also told him to either come down to the kitchen when he was ready or to go to bed, everyone would understand.

When his mom came back down, he hugged her. She told him that she loved him too but did ask why he'd done that. He told her that she was the greatest mother in all the world, and he needed her to know that.

"I thank you, son. I needed that." He said that he did as well. "Good to know that you're not all too big to give your poor old mother hugs." When she went off to the kitchen, Jeffery reached out to his brothers and told them what mom had just said to him. They, too, were going to make it a habit of not just hugging her more but to be around more too. They needed their mother badly and needed to step up their game to make sure she knew it.

He introduced himself to Allen and told him what a fine boy Drew was. "He is. I don't think I'd be here if not for him. That boy. Even when we found his mom's body—well, it gave me nightmares for a few nights just thinking about what she might well have suffered at his hands. I was just telling your family here that we sure have needed someone to help us out."

"This is the family to be with if you need help." Allen said that he could see that. "I'm sure that you've told Edwin about the other Alpha. I want you to know that he won't get to you so long as you're here with us. We protect what we consider family."

He felt that he meant it too. Allen asked if he could rest up a bit, too, and mom took him upstairs as well. Jeffery had a feeling that his mom had just adopted herself another son and grandson to her heart. Since they were all there and it was close to dinner, he and his brothers decided to go get takeout and bring it home. Drew joined them a little while before the food came and looked better now that he'd been given clothing that fit as well as a long shower.

Although he didn't get a mate or a son out of this adventure, Jeffery did feel better than he had this morning when he'd gotten up. He decided that he needed to get out more. Not just dating, though, he did miss that, but he needed to be around more. Not realizing what he'd been missing until today, he was going to pick up his old habit of walking around town in the morning for exercise and enjoy getting to know the people again. It might be all he needed to find himself a mate.

~*~

Sable had all the details that she needed to take care of things. She not only knew what had happened to her family but also a great many details that were going to even shock the Griffin family. She only had to gather them all up in the same place to get things set. While she hadn't any idea what would happen when the truth came out, but she knew that in order for everyone to get on with their lives, especially Patrick and Peter, it had to be brought out. Mostly for Patrick.

Dinner tonight. It was going to happen tonight. As she made sure that everything was where she needed it, Sable also warned Garfield that she would be all right no matter what was said. That he was to please allow her to take care of this. He said he would until blood was shed, then he wasn't making any promises.

"There will be no bloodshed, I promise you this. Once this is finished up, we'll be able to go on that nice trip you and I were talking about." He kissed her. "You're a goof. I love you, but you're still goofy."

When the family started to show up, she was glad she'd had things around they could munch on before the talking started. It was after eight now, and she knew for a fact that they'd all had dinner. But it seemed to her that the Griffins would eat even if they'd only just gotten up from the table. It was a small wonder they all had cooks at their homes.

When Grace showed up, she looked so happy to be there. Sable only hoped that she would be when she started talking. Time would tell, she supposed. Sable kept telling herself that this would be good for all concerned. Peter was the last to arrive after Patrick, and the two of them were cordial to one another. While Peter would have to return to the hospital for more help, he was just as glad to be out of the hospital as she was having this done.

"I'm glad that you all could make it here. I've been doing some research on a few things, and I think it's time it was taken care of." She looked at Grace first. "Do you have anything you'd like to say, Grace? Or should we call you Shirley? Or should I call you mom?"

Grace didn't say anything, but she did pale. When she sat down on the couch, not denying anything that she'd said to her other than to ask her how she'd figured it out. She told her that she'd been figuring out a lot of things since she'd gotten here.

"Like, for instance, Patrick is my biological father. That Belinda and Peter are children that you put in the house for a distraction to each you and Patrick. You took them from an orphanage when they were but children." Grace looked at Patrick. "You thought that with others in the house, you'd not give away your secrets about loving Patrick so that no one would harm him. But it didn't work out that way, did it?"

"No. I loved him, still do and thought that I'd be able to enjoy time with him as 'Shirley' and that would be enough for me. It only made it harder for me to go away when I needed to be the queen of earth." Patrick asked her how she was his child. "You were sleeping one night, and I came to you. It was more than I could have hoped for, being with you that one night. And to have figured out that I was going to have your child was the most wonderful news. But it wasn't to be. There were forces against us that kept tearing at us. Other beings that wanted my power and would do everything to get to me. By using you. So I sent Sable away so that she'd be safe then I continued to be your wife the rest of the time. Bringing Sable to me was a way for me to step down. To be with you."

"Wait. I don't understand. I saw the certificate of when we were born. You and I were twins." Sable told Peter that he was meant to find it. By his looking for her made it all seem real. "So nothing of my life has been true. I'm sorry about your love life and all, but do you have any idea how hard it was to—no, that's not fair to either of you. I've only just realized that you took me from someplace that might well have made me a worse person than I am."

"You were abused there. I had gone there for a female, thinking that she'd be so much like my own daughter that I could have some pain taken away by raising her. But the moment that I saw you, I knew that you needed to be out of there and soon. I only wish that I'd been a better mother to you." Patrick said that he should have been a better father too. "We messed up terribly in doing this to you."

Grace touched her fingers to his face, and Sable saw the exact moment that Peter was healed. He didn't move or lash out, asking why it had taken someone so long but cried. Sobbed his thankfulness to Grace for giving him this chance.

"I'm going to be a better man. I am. I've been thinking of all the things that I've done in the name of magic and my pursuit for it that I'm ashamed of myself for it." Peter looked at her. "I'm going to continue to be the person that you said I needed to be in order to heal myself. Because even though I can walk and be a man again, I'm not nearly healed. I need to get my head and my heart in the right place in order to feel that way. Thank you for that."

"I'm glad to hear that, Peter. And when you're ready, because I know you're not right now, you and I will get to know each other despite not being blood-related." Sable turned to the others in the room. "Belinda is going to go to prison. For a long time. I've taken care that she will age like other humans and die when the time comes for her. Peter has been helpful in telling me the things that he remembers her bragging on that she'd done to humans and fae alike."

"I'm proud of you, son. And even though we're not related, I'd like to get to know you like a man would his son. I've been negligent in doing that for either of you. I want to do that now." Peter told Patrick that he'd like that as well. "I feel like I've been given a second chance. Grace, will you be my wife? I've wanted you to be my wife since the first time I laid eyes on you. I'll be right there with you every step of the way to keep you and your kingdom safe too. I'm sure that Garfield here will keep Sable safer than we can. But you'd do me a great honor if you were to consent to allowing me to be your mate for all time."

"Yes, I'd love that. Forever. It will cause some uproar around the magical world, but I think with our daughter helping us, we can be assured of being a lasting king and queen of all the land." Patrick sat down next to Grace and held her hand. This next part was going to be a little more difficult for everyone. "Go on, Sable. Whatever you have to tell us, we'll get through it as a family now."

"All right. Three nights ago, someone from your household allowed a group of people onto the magical land. As I've never been acknowledged as your child until today, I wasn't able to take care that they were moved off. The person, the faerie that did this, is here, bound and gagged so that you can deal with him as well. It's Boo." Grace looked at the small creature when she pulled him out of the tall cabinet that held books. "He's been trying to get to you since the day that I was born. He knew, you see, that you and I were mother and daughter. He's been, I guess you could call it, feeding them information about your daily activities for some time now. Since, at least, from the time I was born."

"Boo? Are you — well, of course, you are. Did he give you a reason?" Grace looked at the cage and ordered him to be released from the magic that had put him in the small cell-like box. Once he was free, he flew toward Grace to what they all assumed was to attack her. Patrick was able to grab him before he could do any damage. Even though he's a small faerie, he would have hurt her badly with his nails and hands. "What have you done? What have I done to deserve such violence from you? For that matter, why would you do this to anyone? You've been treated so well, Boo, that —"

"Well? You think that I've been treated well? I have not. I've been in a prison of your making, watching over your bastard daughter for decades without any thought to what I might have wanted to do. I have no home of my own. No wife with children of her. You took that all away from me when you set me about to watching your child that had more magic than I did. From her very birth." She told him he could have come to her, and she would have made other arrangements. "I did. Threefold. You told me that I was doing such a fine job of it that you doubted that anyone could take my place. I didn't want to do this at all, can't you see? I thought that if I could get her hurt badly or even you, you'd see my point. What it was like to have no one in my life because of you."

"Enough." It was Patrick that spoke and had Boo bowing before him as if he were already king to him. "You were given an assignment and knowing Grace as well as I do, I'm sure you were asked to do it and not ordered. Were you?"

"What would have happened to me should I have turned her down? She would have killed me." Grace told Boo that she would have found someone else. "No. No. You did this to me, and I'll not hear your excuses for it. You deserve whatever I can let happen to you. You did this."

"Nay, you did this on your own." Everyone turned to Garfield when he spoke. His voice, while quiet, held a great deal of anger in it. "You wanted to be a martyr in all this, didn't you, Boo? It had occurred to you a great deal that if anyone would have hurt Sable, then you'd be blessed with such a good life when you returned back to the castle. Isn't that right? All the things you made a list for." The small paper was tossed at him by Garfield. "That was your plan. Not to have either of them *pay* for you being assigned a job that anyone else would have done happily, but you wanted Sable to be hurt, you as well, so that you'd be taken care of for the rest of your long life."

"It would have worked too if not for the fact that Sable was forever finding out what I had planned. Not me, the planner, but when someone came to the house to do my bidding. Christ, do you have any idea how many times I tried to make it happen to her? For me? So many that I cannot compare it to the stars in the sky. It is so many. To the flowers in the spring. She was forever—I hate her for that." Garfield turned to Grace and then knelt before her before speaking.

"He wished to harm my mate. My mate that

I love so much more than I could have hoped for. I would if you'd allow it see to his punishment for what he might well have done to her." Grace looked at her, then back at Garfield. "If it would help you decide, my lady, I promise you he will not suffer, but he will pay."

"So be it." She was as startled as the rest of the room when Garfield simply thanked Grace, then turned and smashed Boo into the table he'd been on. Sable couldn't imagine the strength it would have taken him to do such a thing. To kill a faerie isn't as easy as some would think. But Garfield had done it for her.

Sable couldn't have been more in love with this man than she was at that moment. Going to him, she held to him as she told him how much she loved him. Garfield turned to who she supposed were her parents now that she thought about it and smiled at them.

"I will forever pledge myself to you when my brother has no need for my services." Edwin said he would pledge his pack to the queen should she need it as well. "I only ask that you allow Sable and me a way that we can come and visit the two of you on the other realm. And any children Sable would like to have with me as well."

"There is nothing that I would like better than that. In fact, I think we should make it so that all your family can come to the castle as well. It would certainly make my heart sing to have pretty wolves around again. They have come to this land to be with Edwin and his pack because he is such a good man." Edwin thanked her for her kind words. "They are truly spoken, my alpha. You are a good leader, as much so as your father was during his time. I thank you for your wanting to be a part of my land as well."

After she was finished with her revelations about what she'd found, most of it anyway, Edwin asked Grace—mom—if she could locate an alpha for him. While they were there with their heads together, Sable noticed that Peter and Patrick were making plans to move into the old home together to get to know each other. No words were spoken about Belinda, and Sable thought that to be very telling as to how much trouble she'd caused for everyone. Sable sat down next to Luna and took her hand into hers.

"Drew will need a mother's hand to help guide him. When this is finished with the other alpha, he'll need someone too that will help him through the changes that he'll need as well. Charlie will be a good person for that too." She asked if she could see that in the future. "No. I know he'll need you more than anyone could guess right now. He will need to grieve for his mother too. I can't think of a person that would help him with that process better than you. You'd be the grandmother he wouldn't ever have without you."

"You're going to adopt him then." She said that she'd have to adopt Allen too, and she thought him much too old to be having a mother ordering him around. "I suppose that's true enough. But I will take them both into my heart and keep them on their toes."

"Thank you for that." Once people started leaving, going to their respective homes, she sat on the couch with Garfield.

"You did a good job. I hope that you don't mind that I destroyed Boo. I know you promised me that no blood would be shed, but he didn't deserve to live, not after what he'd plotted and planned for you." She told him that she thought that Grace would return him to her realm and be destroyed there. But she also thought his way was much more humane than Grace would have given him. "Yes. Now that you say that, I think you might be right. How about you and I go up and try to kill one another again? I'll even allow you to come as many times as you wish."

"Big promise there when you know that you do that already." They were both laughing as they made their way to their bedroom. "I'd like to have children with you, Garfield. As many as we can. I don't even care if we adopt a houseful of them, so long as we can love them like we want."

"Deal." He picked her up, taking her down the hall to their bedroom. Sable couldn't wait to hold a child in her arms. She wanted that as badly as she wanted Garfield to give it to her.

Chapter 6

Sable loved the way Garfield touched her. Just a simple touch of his fingers to her arm would set off small tremors throughout her body. When he touched his lips to her throat, she would have to stiffen her legs so as not to collapse on the floor in a puddle of putty. And his kisses would make her weak. Not just in her body but her mind too. The man was lethal when it came to making love to her.

"You have the most extraordinary taste to your skin. It reminds me of blossoms in the spring." She couldn't make a comment to him, even if she had one to offer. Her mouth had dried up, and her tongue tangled around her words. "Sable, everything about you has me drawing on memories of my lifetime. The color of your hair is that of the fall leaves that crunch under my boot when I walk over them. The rosy color of your lips is akin to the blooms of the roses in my mother's garden. Oh, how I love you."

Garfield picked her up then, pressing her body to his as he pressed her back to the wall behind them. Telling her to strip for him, it was all she could do not to beg him to do the same. Once her clothing was gone, he looked down at her breasts.

She felt his cock at her entrance. He was thick and hard. As he watched her, his hands were all over her back, ribs, and breasts. Her body was on fire, and her breasts ached with need. When Garfield lifted her up so that her breasts were at the level of his mouth, she cried out, clinging to his body while he nibbled and suckled at her.

"More." He just grinned at her. "You're killing me, Garfield. I need more. Don't tease me. Please?"

"I want you so needy that you come without me taking you." She thought that wouldn't be too difficult as close to the edge as she was now. "Come for me, Sable. Come with me just taking your nipple into my mouth."

As soon as he took the pebbled bud into his mouth, she screamed out her release. Her body shook from it. The rawness of her primal need being met was such a relief that she was limp again. But almost as soon as she came a second time, she was ready again, her need to release making her body hurt and ache with unfulfillment. Grabbing his hair and pulling him from her nipples, Sable kissed Garfield with all the savagery that she was feeling.

He didn't just put her down on the floor then, but he stepped back from her, his own body shaking. Had he not steadied her before putting his arms at his side, she might well have fallen down. She was so weak with it. But it was the immediate hurt that had her smacking his hands away from her when he reached for her a second time.

"You're in heat. Ovulating, I mean." Sable looked at him confused, her mind still a bit wobbly from coming so hard. "Having sex now would most assuredly fill you with our child. I know that you said you wanted children, but I wanted you to know that you would be getting pregnant if I were to come inside of you right now."

"I'm not on any kind of protection." He said that it wouldn't matter once he came inside of her. She'd be pregnant. "All right. What do you think of us creating a child today? I'd like to know exactly how you feel about having a baby with me so soon after meeting."

"I would love to see you heavy with our child. Also, you need to be aware that it might not be a single child. We could have two or three just as easily as having one." She thought she'd heard that someplace but nodded at him. "It's your body, Sable. If you want to wait, now is the time to tell me. I'll still enjoy your body and make sure that you enjoy it as well. But it's entirely up to you if we create a child."

"I want a child with you. I don't care...well, I guess I would care if we had fifty, but I want children with you. Now would be a good start." He pulled her gently to him then, kissing her as if she were a fragile flower that he didn't want to crush. When he put his forehead to hers, she smiled at him. "You're going to be the most wonderful father, Garfield. But if we don't have sex right now, I'm going to have to find some other way of coming because you're taking too long."

When he picked her up in both arms and sent her sailing through the air, she squealed in delight. Bouncing twice on the big bed, she didn't get to move out of his way when he joined her. The kiss he gave her this time was loving, wonderfully thorough. Flipping him to his back, she settled over his hips and fisted his cock while she tried to figure out how to ride him this way.

"Let me help you." Giving her instructions on how she was to get up on her knees, he held his cock while she slowly, ever so wonderfully, slid down over his thickness and sat on his groin. "Christ, don't move just yet. If you do, then I'm going to come quickly, and I'd like to watch you get your enjoyment like this."

She rolled her hips. Sable didn't know who growled the loudest when she did that, him or her. But the feeling of having him at her leisure was more than she could have begged for. Getting a rhythm going, she rode his cock. Garfield put her hands at her breasts, and she cupped them in her hands, pushing them up to her mouth so that her tongue could tease her hard nipple. Garfield nearly knocked her to the floor, rolling her to her back and fucking her hard.

Coming so many times like this, his taking her hard, she knew that she was going to be sore. And nothing about that thought made her want to stop him. When he bowed back, his wolf running over his skin, she watched as he howled out to the room and came.

She felt every drop of his cum filling her. Coming with him, screaming out her releases, she couldn't help but watch him as he came two more times deep inside of her. Sable felt the bed, or perhaps the earth move under her and blacked out.

Waking alone in the middle of the big bed, she heard Garfield in the bathroom. The shower was on, but he was talking to someone. Just as she entered the room, getting up slowly as her body was hurting a little more than she had anticipated, he was sitting on the commode with his cell phone to his ear. When she asked him if everything was all right, he nodded and then shook his head.

While he finished up his conversation, she stepped into the warm shower. For a few minutes, she just let the water flow over her as it helped loosen her muscles. When Garfield joined her while she was washing her hair, she asked him again if everything was all right.

"They found the other alpha. He's from Virginia and is now in this territory without notifying Edwin as to why he's here. Or, for that matter, that he's here at all." She asked him what was going to happen now. "Both Edwin and Storm will confront him about being here. Then they're both within their right to have him killed. I don't know that it will come to that, but since both Allen and Drew have asked to join Edwin's pack, anything that happens to the two of them will be certain death for the man. By the way, there is a pack meeting on Monday night. Edwin wants us all to be there with him so that everyone can meet the newest members of his pack."

"How big is his pack? I have a feeling that it's not a small one. I don't know why but that's the feeling that I have." Garfield finished washing her back before answering her. "Six thousand? That's a lot of members. I'm assuming that it's the entire state that he runs."

"He is nearly the only alpha in Ohio, yes. There are a couple of smaller packs around the area, but since he's a good guy and a great leader, Edwin will more than likely get those under his protection sooner or later." Once they were showered and feeling better, they made their way down to the kitchen. "I'm starving. I hope we have something to snack on before dinner."

"Snacking is an understatement where you guys are concerned. I've seen you guys eat what would be to a normal person an entire meal before sitting down to have a huge dinner." He said that his wolf needed more energy. "Sure. That's it. You stick with that one for as long as you can. I'm sure someday that all this snacking, as you call it, catches up with you."

Garfield let out a bark of laughter. "Are you saying that I'll get too big for my wolf to chase his mate down?" She said that she was saying that exactly. "We can't put on weight as an immortal. To be honest with you, I don't think I've ever seen a fat wolf ever. Now, while you're carrying our child, you will gain some weight, but it won't stick around for long after you give birth." It hit her then that she was going to have a baby.

Putting her hands over her still flat belly, she had about a million questions go through her head all at once. She knew how a baby worked for humans. The usual amount of time that they carried a child. How big one would be. But as for a wolf, she hadn't a clue. The next time she had some free time, she was going to go talk to Luna. It might be less embarrassing to go to her than to rely on Garfield or one of the others to help her with answers.

Going to work wasn't something that she was enjoying as much as she used to. Now it was taking time from her family. Mostly it was Garfield, but she was missing spending time with not just her parents but Peter too. She wondered as she sat down to work if he was still on the track of being a different person than he was before. Only time would tell, she supposed.

Investing had been something that came naturally to her. She'd never thought of it as cheating the system. Just because she knew what was going to be a winner or not didn't mean that she was cheating someone out of their money. Sable was careful not to invest too much into some of the things that she worked with. She noticed, too, that Garfield did the same. He was careful what he put his money into and didn't do it where they would lose their shirts if it was a bust.

"May I talk to you?" She smiled at Drew when he came into her office. "You were working so hard I didn't think you heard me when I knocked."

"I didn't. What can I do for you? Are you getting to know the others in the pack?" He said he was going out there today with Allen to check it out. "Good. I want reviews on the place myself. I might be sending my own kids there someday." She had a feeling that he knew she was breeding, as Garfield called it, before he left the house. "What can I do for you?"

"Allen and I don't have a car. I'm not asking you to give us one, but I was wondering if it would be all right to borrow one from one of the people here. I won't be driving in case you thought I meant that." She smiled at him and told him she hadn't thought of that. "Allen is a good driver. He isn't overly cautious like my mom used to be. And I promise you we won't make a habit of borrowing it. But I need some school supplies and also some clothing. So does Allen. I think too that he wants a job when he's feeling better."

"I think we can work something out about the car and the job. How is he feeling? Better, I'm assuming." Drew told her he naps a lot but not as much as he used to. "Garfield told me that as soon as this mess is taken care of with the other alpha, then he'll heal right away. As for the car, you and Allen can borrow mine whenever you need it. Everything that I need is within walking distance around here, and I can get a ride with Garfield when I need to go beyond where I think I can walk. Have Allen come by the house later, and he can just take it home with you. I'm not using it, and it's a shame to let it just sit there and not be used when someone can use it."

"I'll tell him. He doesn't know that I'm here. But I'm sort of nervous about getting out too much. I'm afraid of getting caught." Sable told him she would be as well. Drew stood up when she did. "I'll let him know that you said he could come and get the car. Thanks, bunches, Aunt Sable."

He was gone before she could wonder why he'd called her aunt. She loved that he wanted to and did it, but she did have to wonder if he called the rest of the family aunt or uncle. Getting back to work, she was in a better frame of mind after her visit. Maybe she'd hire him to come by and distract her once a day. It had only been a few minutes, but it was just what she needed.

~*~

Rocky was getting frustrated. And when he was

frustrated, he tended to snap out at people and hurt them. Not that it gave him much pause in keeping himself in check. Right now, it would have thrilled him to no end to find someone, preferably a woman, to take it out on. He looked around the area where he could still smell the boy.

He knew his name was Andrew, but he'd been calling him *boy* since he'd taken over the pack about a year ago. It had irked the kid so much that he even got into an argument with him. That had cost the boy dearly. He might well have been nursing that bloody lip for more than a week after he was finished with him. Then there was his mother. Christ, he had wanted her so badly that he had sent his own mate out of town for a week just so he could take his time in wooing her. But she still wouldn't submit.

Another time his anger got the better of him. Rocky wasn't sure at what point he'd lost his temper because she was fighting him. But he'd not just broken her neck, but he'd beaten her so badly that it had been difficult for him to even look at her. If she'd just done what he told her to do and not pulled out that gun, he might well have let her go.

"No, I wouldn't have." Laughing at his own little inside joke, he knew as surely as he was standing here that he would have killed his own mate to have Isabella in his bed nightly. Hell, he'd be hard-pressed to leave the bed at all if he had her at his command. But she never gave up. Even drawing first blood from him.

The place where she'd scratched him with her claw still hurt. It wasn't bleeding as badly as it had been when she'd cut him. The only reason that he could think that he'd not bled out was the fact that he was an alpha. Otherwise, he might well have died by now.

"Can I help you?" He turned when a woman's voice called out from behind him. Christ, Ohio had the best-looking woman in the world, he thought to himself. "What or who are you looking for, moron?"

"Excuse me? You can't talk to me like that. I'm not going to stand for it." She just snorted at him. "You'd best be saying how sorry you are for insulting me, or I'm going to have to hurt you."

"Oh yeah? Good luck with that. Who the fuck are you sniffing around for, Rocky? It wouldn't be Allen or Drew, would it?" It took him a moment to remember that it was their names. "It's not very bright of you to come into someone else's playpen and not advise them that you are there, is it? I mean, you didn't even bother looking to see what the alpha around here is called, did you?"

"Who the fuck do you think you are, talking to me like that?" Again she snorted at him. Coming down off the porch of the house that he had thought Allen and the boy were in, he noticed that she was better looking than he first thought. Fuckable too. "You, by chance, have the key to this place? You and I could have us a good time if you do. Not that it matters if we fuck each other in a bed or on the ground. I'll make it good for you."

"No, you won't. And you'll not touch me either. My mate will have you for—damn it. I forgot to tell you who I was. Pardon me. My name is Storm Griffin. My mate and alpha is Edwin Griffin. You might want to remember that when asked later." He was the one that snorted this time. "You don't think that's an impressive thing? To be confronted by the alpha's mate?"

"Alpha bitch." She said that she was both, yes. "No. I mean, that's what you're called. The alpha bitch. If you were mine, I'd make sure you went only by that name. You're not going to go far with the way you're acting towards me, little girl. Wait until I come here and take the pack from your—"

The hand on his shoulder had him reaching up and digging his claws into it. Instead of begging to be let go, the person retaliated by digging his own nails into his shoulder. Christ, it hurt. Turning around, he knew that on all kinds of levels that he'd bitten off a good deal more than he could handle with this one.

"What were you saying to my wife?" He said that he'd only been teasing her. "Sure you were. I suppose a better question would be is, why are you in my territory, and I've not been notified of it? You've been sniffing around for the last few days. Plenty of time for you to have called the pack office and made yourself known to me."

"I guess I let it slip my mind. But since I have you here. I'm looking for a man and a boy. Allen and Andrew are their names." The man, Griffin, he supposed his name was asked him for more details than that. Like a last name. "I had it written down, but I left the notes at the house I'm staying in."

"You're not staying in a house around here,

so why don't you try again. You've been living out of your car for the past month while you hunt them down." What the hell was this man doing, having him watched? "I am, as a matter of fact. Having you watched, I mean. Answer my question."

"I don't know their last name. I know that Allen is a pussy, and that boy is nothing but trouble." Griffin just crossed his arms over his chest. A mighty impressive chest too. "I'm taking them back to my pack so they can stand judgement for a few things that I know they've been up to."

"Really? Well, I guess it sucks that you've come all this way and won't be able to take them back with you. Allen Dresher pledged himself and Drew Bailey as his adopted son to my pack just this morning." Rocky said that wasn't possible as he owned them. "Owned them? How is that possible? Alphas don't own the people that he protects. Unless you have that all wrong and you're protecting yourself. They said that you killed Drew's mother when she wouldn't have sex with you."

"See right there, that's a bald-faced lie. I'm telling you, there isn't anyone around to trust anymore. You just hand them over to me, and I'll see to their punishment for you. In fact, it would be my—"

"Shut the fuck up." Rocky felt the power run over his body when the woman snapped her fingers at him and told him to sit. It wasn't a matter of him sitting but how quickly he could. While on the ground, he felt the need to submit to the bigger man. "You wouldn't last a day as one of our pack members."

"Yeah? Is that what you think?" Rocky couldn't get his mouth to shut up. It was like his brain and mouth weren't on the same page about keeping him from getting killed. "I could be a member of this pack in no time."

"I accept." Not understanding what Griffin meant, he sat there for several very short seconds until his body caught up with the man's acceptance. "You're not a member of my pack."

His body began to twist and churn. It felt like he was being sucked through his ass hole and turned inside out. Even as he screamed out in pain, he knew the worst was yet to come. When his status as alpha was taken from him, Rocky felt every wound, every muscle ache that he'd ever had as a man. And it was ten times worse than he'd ever felt because that was the way the magic worked. Ten times what you give to someone else.

Lying on the ground, blood and sweat all over him, he couldn't even muster up the energy to look up at the couple that had pulled this from him. When his name was said twice, it took it before it registered that they were speaking to him before he could move enough to look up at his new alpha.

"You are hereby judged by me on the murder of Isabella Bailey, mother of Andrew Bailey, mate to Allen Dresher. Before I pass judgment on you, Rockland Jamison, I will inform you that your ill-gotten gains from stealing from your own people have been removed from all your accounts. Both here and overseas." He told him that was his. The kick to his groin had him falling backwards onto the ground. "You were not given permission to speak. The people in the pack that you nearly ruined with your greed and ill-treatment will be able to go to another pack without any trouble. They will also be given a portion of the money that was taken from you. The money you stole from them in the first place. Is there anything you wish to say that will be the truth?"

"You bastard. I'm going to get you." This time the kick came from the woman. Trying to grab her leg when she hit him in the head was futile. She was as quick as a rabbit. "You're going to regret this. See that you don't."

"I won't." He saw the boy coming out from behind a line of wolves. The four of them were huge, and Rocky had no doubt they were related to the alpha. Their fur was standing on end, and their teeth were bared. "Drew, do you have something to say to this man? Now is the time before I pass judgement on him."

"Is he going to die?" he was interested in the answer to that question too. When Griffin told the boy that he was going to die for sure, he wondered how that was going to come about. Didn't anyone remember that there had to be a trail? That he would be allowed to have his day in court? He'd see to that. "Then I'd like to take from him the exact thing he took from me."

The boy stood before him, and Rocky laughed. "What do you think you're going to do to me, boy? Nothing, that's what. When I get your little ass back to my pack land, I'm going to teach you a lesson that you're never going to forget."

"I'm no longer afraid of you." The slash to his throat startled him. Putting his hands up around his throat, he tried his best to stop the flow of blood that was squirting from his veins. "That was for my mother that you killed. This is for hurting my dad."

The second slash to his neck had Rocky thinking that his head was no longer attached to his body. Blood was flowing out of him at too rapid of a flow for him to think that he was going to walk away from this at all. As he fell backward, his body no longer strong enough to hold him up, Rocky looked at the booted feet as they did nothing, not a thing to help him. He did watch as the boy just turned his back on him and walked away.

Coughing was making his blood spurt out of him quicker. But there didn't seem to be a way for him to stop it. Rocky could no longer feel his feet or legs. His arms no longer held his head to his shoulders. He was, in a few words, about dead. And there was shit that he could do about it.

The weaker he got, the more he wanted to say. It wasn't until he heard the howling that he knew he was as good as dead. And the idiots surrounding him were having a good old fashion howling to celebrate. It was a beautiful sound if he did say so himself. It was a nice sound to be lulled to death by.

Finding himself in the afterlife where all alphas were supposed to go, he knew that he'd be welcome here if nowhere else. They had to accept him. Had to allow him to be in this realm with all the others pack leaders. As he was looking around for someone to show him around, what he had heard all his life would happen, he noticed that the area surrounding him was turning a deep shade of blood red. The man that stood before him turned his nose up at him before Rocky was able to put out his hand to be welcomed.

"You aren't welcome here." He said that he was, in fact, going to be welcome. He was a powerful alpha. "You aren't anything. You were killed by a child because you murdered his mother. Nay, you are not welcome here. I will send you along where other monsters stay in a moment. However, there is one person here that wishes to speak to you."

Isabella stood before him. Even in death, she was a goddess. Trying to stand up, his body not cooperating with him, he just watched her as she walked around him. Then when she threw back her head and laughed, he wondered what she found so funny.

"He killed you. My son got revenge for you killing me. I couldn't be more prouder of him than I am at this moment." Rocky told her she should be ashamed of what he'd done to him. "No, I think not. I'm ashamed I couldn't kill you myself, but this is much better. Drew avenged his mother. There isn't a better thing to happen than this."

"Why are you here? You're no more an alpha than that boy of yours is." She said that she was an alpha. Had been since birth. And her plans were to run a good pack until he came along. "Well, you should be thanking me then. Women are only good for one thing, and that's fucking. You should have learned that by now."

"Be gone." He didn't know what was happening, but he felt himself tumble backwards. Even as he fell, for what felt like miles, he knew that he was not going to be in a good place. The darkness of the area he was headed to was like a deep hole. Rocky couldn't stand the darkness, and he had a feeling that that was precisely why he'd been sent here. Once he stopped moving, he felt the dark obscurity of his new home swallow him up. Rocky was in deep trouble here, and he was terrified that he wasn't going to get any reprieve for the next million years. If not forever.

Chapter 7

Garfield was still sitting at his desk, doing nothing but thinking about Drew. Everyone had been so shocked at his killing Rocky that even Edwin had been at a loss for words. According to Storm, Drew wasn't going to face any charges for killing a pack member as he'd been sentenced to death beforehand. It still amazed him that a ten year old boy had killed someone so quickly and seemingly without any nightmares about doing it.

Getting up when the doorbell rang, he welcomed Allen into his house. Sable had left an hour ago, and he wasn't expecting her for another hour or two. Mom was helping her with having their child, and he wanted her to remember everything she told her so she could tell him.

Inviting Allen into the kitchen to have a drink with him, Garfield was hoping he wasn't here for questions about Drew. He didn't have any answers. Edwin didn't even have them. The kid was going down in history as the bravest man-child he knew, that was for sure.

"I need your help with some money." Garfield told him he'd do whatever he needed for him. "Thank you. As you may or may not know, because Rocky killed Isabella, Drew and I were given a great deal of money. Also, I was finally able to claim the insurance policy that she'd taken out on herself when her husband died. I was the benefactor on that one. But I want Drew to have it."

"You want me to invest it for the two of you." Allen said that he didn't want Drew to have to work while going to college. He wanted him to get a good education with the money. "All right. But you are aware that you're a part of our family as much as I am, correct? Drew is already calling my brothers uncle and their wives aunt. Even my parents are being called grandparents."

"Yes, I'm aware of that. It was all his doing, but I think it's best for him and me too." Garfield asked him if anyone had talked to him about being a part of the Griffin family. "I mean, they welcomed me into the pack and said that we're family too. But I don't know what you mean about anything else."

"You're an immortal." He shook his head. "Yes, you are. You and Drew both are. Drew will stop aging when he hits about twenty-five, then he'll just be like us."

"I don't understand. Like you?" He told him that he was an ancient. "I'm sorry. Perhaps I'm being dense. What do you mean by that?"

"My dad was alive during a time when the state wasn't even called Ohio. He lived through wars when they began in the seventeen hundreds. By then, my dad and my mom both were thousands of years old. Myself and my brothers were born to them during the beginning of their life together. All of us are old and have seen things that would boggle your mind." Allen said that wasn't possible. "It is, and it's the truth. I can't lie to you, Allen. Not that I would, but I'm telling you the truth." He got up to pace.

"I'm not saying you're lying to me, but how is that even remotely possible? I mean, not to dismiss your claims of...do you have any idea how young you look?" Garfield laughed. "This isn't funny. You're older than dirt, my boy."

"Yes, well, I suppose you might be right on that. But I wanted to tell you that so you'd understand that with age comes magic. And as you know, Storm and her sister, along with Jana, brought a great deal of magic to us as well. We're powerful, Allen, and so are you now." He asked him if that had anything to do with him being able to change his clothing with a thought. "Yes. I bet that scared you a bit. I know it did me when I realized I could do it."

"I was in a dressing room when it happened. I thought I'd like the blue shirt better than the gray one and I was suddenly wearing it. I asked Drew about it, and he acted like it was something he'd been doing since birth." They both laughed. "I'm sorry. I'm sure you were making a point about telling me this."

"I did. You won't ever die, Allen, nor will Drew. You won't have to worry about being sick, having cancer or anything else that might take you from us.

We've been around for a long time, so we have a great deal of money. And so long as we have money, you'll have it too." He said that they needed a house. "Oh shit. I forgot. Here is the deed to the house you were living in when we found you. It's bought and paid for, and there are accounts opened for you, too, all over town. If you want to get rid of any of the things in the house, we ask that you donate them to a charity of your choice."

"This is too much." Garfield said that it was what family did for one another. Allen looked over the paperwork. "It says that there is a car and truck in the garage. Also a staff. I don't think we need all that."

"You'll be surprised at how handy a cook will be for you when Drew starts to fill out his wolf. It's an endless job of feeding him. Trust me, I know. The staff will help you too in keeping you both fed and safe. While you can't die, you can be kidnapped. We don't want that to happen either." Allen said that he didn't either. "Then you'll keep the staff around?"

"Yes. I'd be more afraid for Drew than for myself, in that matter." Garfield didn't point out that Drew was a wolf and, therefore, better at slipping away, but

Allen was speaking again. "I need to find a job. If for no other reason than to keep me busy. I've worked all my life, and just because we've had a windfall, I don't want to sit around idle."

"There are plenty of jobs within the family that you can take over for us at any time." Thanking him, Garfield watched as Allen paced. "I have a sister that I'd like to bring here sometime. I've had her staying away so she'd not get hurt if or when Rocky found us. Even before Isabella was murdered, I was fearful of her coming around."

"You bring her around, and we'll make sure she has everything she needs as well." Allen said she had three daughters, triplets that she was raising on her own. "That's terrible for her, but when she gets here, there is plenty of family around to help her out with them. How old are they?"

"Six. Blond hair, blue eyes. Just the cutest little girls you've ever seen. She's never been married. The guy who fathered them was married, and Paige didn't know. Once she told him about the baby, she hadn't been aware of them being triplets by then, he told her that she needed to get rid of them because he didn't want his wife to know. As you can imagine, that didn't go over very well for her." Garfield laughed with Allen again. "I want to bring her here so she can finally have a permanent roof over her head. Food that doesn't come from a can, and the girls have more than just one dress a year to wear when they go out. I want the best for them as much as I do for Drew."

"Drew wants you to adopt him. Did you know that?" He said that they'd been talking about it. "Good. When you make a decision, let Storm know, and she'll put the paperwork in for you. It will be a done deal then." He thanked him again, but Allen seemed distracted. "Anything else I need to help you with? I'm here for you, Allen."

"Can you go with me to get her? I have this strange feeling that I need to go right now to bring her here." Garfield stood up, telling him to always act on those feelings. "We're going now?"

"Yes. Now. I only need to let Sable know, and we'll be going." They were on the road in ten minutes. Paige only lived in Cincinnati, but it was an eight-hour drive there and back. Since they were bringing four people back with them and who knew what else,

Garfield rented them a cargo van to drive so they could be comfortable with them all riding together. By the time they reached Middletown, he knew as much about Paige as he did any other member of the family.

The drive was uneventful but boring. Drew, at the last minute, decided to go with them, and it was good for him to be helping out too. Stopping to get some burgers when they reached Jeffersonville. Trading driving with Allen, Garfield was happy to sit on the other side of the car.

It was nearly dinner time when they pulled onto the street that Paige lived on. The longer they drove down the street toward her home, the worse the houses got. He was almost afraid when they pulled up in front of a sorry-looking duplex that looked like it should have been torn down with the other places around it. Getting out, Garfield kept an eye on their surroundings as Allen went to the door and knocked.

"Oh, dear god." Forgetting his fear for the sound of Allen's voice, Garfield took off toward the house after telling Drew to stay in the car. As soon as he was only a few feet from the door where Allen was standing, he could smell the blood. "Help me, Garfield. I think she's been shot."

Calling an ambulance was a priority. Even as the police pulled up in front of the house, he could see people coming out of their homes to see what was going on. The ambulance arrived ten minutes after the police had, and that had been a long time in coming too. Garfield was pissed off when one of the medics told him that they don't usually come out this time of night to this area. It's too dangerous.

"So what do you do, leave them to die out here because you don't take your job seriously enough to care?" The man told him to back off, or he'd be in the next ambulance. "I'd like to see you try that. Come on. Show me what you have."

"Uncle Garfield." Stretching his neck, hearing it pop, he told Drew he was sorry. "It's all right to me, but you're scaring the girls."

By the time Paige and one of her daughters were being taken away, he had the other two finding things they wanted to take with them. He was glad when he saw the packed bags that Allen had called his sister when they started out to tell her to get ready.

It didn't take them long to get loaded up. The

house, despite it being such a dump on the outside, looked very nice on the inside. It was clean though worn out. The fridge didn't work, so there was a cooler with ice on the floor with milk and eggs in it. There was very little else in the house to speak of in the way of food.

"Do you know what happened?" Allen said he'd tell him later. He then reminded him about their link. Allen said he was too pissed off to talk right now and just looked out the window. Reaching for Storm, he told her what was going on as well as what they encountered when they arrived.

"Give me a moment here. I'm hacking into the police station now. I'll also take care to find out about the medics telling you that. I have a feeling that things are going to get worse before — here it is. The call came in two hours ago. Two fucking hours and they only just arrived when you got there? Heads are going to be looped off. You can bet on that. Anyway, it says here that a child called in that her mother had been shot and that she needed someone to come to the house. There were noises in the background that the 911 operator noted in his notes. Screams, as well as a loud male voice. Two shots were fired while he was on the line with

the child, and he hung up on her. When she called back, she got a different operator who told her not to call in again. I'm telling you right now, Garfield, I'm going to take Rain with me, and we're going to fucking clean house down there."

"Just tell me what you found, honey, so I can take care that none of the others are hurt." She said she didn't like to be calm about what happened. *"I'm not either. But we really need to get this taken care of in an order."*

"One of the little girls said it was the landlord that hurt her mother and sister. She said that mom had been trying to keep up with the rent, but he kept changing the price, and her mom was trying." She read the notes on the incident and then told Garfield what she'd been able to find in the archives.

"So she's been having issues with her landlord for some time, and without the police coming around when she calls, he thinks he can get away with whatever he wants. Please tell me that you're going to find him for me." She told him that she was going to find him for her. *"Just be careful that you don't leave enough evidence around that you get caught."*

"Did you just tell me that I can go ahead and kill this prick so long as I'm careful? I think I love you more than

Edwin right now." He smiled, knowing that his brother wouldn't find that to be funny in the least bit. *"Rain and I are going to come there now. You just take care that the little family is all right. Bring them here if you can tonight, and we'll make sure that they have a better life."*

"That's what Allen and I were talking about when he asked me to come with him. His sister has had a rough life, it seems. Well, we're in front of the hospital now. I'll let you know what I know here in a little while." He entered the mostly full emergency department and had to ask three times as to where Paige and her daughter were. *"I need you to do something for me, Storm. They're not going to operate on either of them because they don't have insurance. I know that's against the law, but I'm thinking that so long as they treat the wounds, that's all they have to do. Can you get some asses rolling so that they can be fixed up enough for me to bring them home so that they can get proper care?"*

He knew that he sounded pissed off. He was about as pissed as he'd ever been in his life. When the phone rang next to the desk he was standing by, Garfield knew the moment that someone was getting their ass reamed by Storm. After she hung up, the nurse ran around telling people to get their asses in gear and help the Dresher family. He was going to have to get Storm a big gift for helping him in this.

Removing the bullet wasn't a long surgery. However, once they got her into surgery and took some x-rays, they found broken ribs. Another bullet hole in her back, as well as enough cuts and scratches on her body that totaled about two hundred stitches. The little girl, Amy, didn't fare much better than her mother.

She also had broken ribs. A busted lip that required stitches both inside and outside her mouth. And trauma to the back of her head. Had she laid there overnight with the wound to her head, the surgeon told him she would have died. As it was, Garfield gave them both a bit of his blood to help them along to being well enough to take home.

Taking the other two girls to a hotel, knowing they'd be in the hospital overnight, they ordered pizza for them all and watched some television. Allen kept the girls eating, and they were asleep as soon as he put them to bed. Stress could do that, he knew firsthand.

"She's going to be all right, you think?" Garfield told him he'd give her more of his magic if she didn't look good in the morning. "Thank you for that. I was talking to Libby, and she said that Mr. Hopewell comes by once a month trying to get into her mom's pants. I'm not sure she understands what that means, but she knows enough to hate the man on site."

They talked about getting them home and what was going to happen when they got there. He heard from Rain once and Storm twice. Mr. Hopewell wasn't going to be a problem anymore, and he would never be found. He didn't ask though he wanted to know what they'd done. He was just happy that it had been taken care of.

Garfield didn't sleep much. He was thinking about how some men, and he knew women, could treat the opposite sex. His parents would have skinned him alive, literally, if he'd tried anything like what he'd witnessed tonight. Or, for that matter, over the past few weeks. He was going to make it a point to keep an eye out for happenings like this one from now on.

"I've sent the plane to bring you all home. Paige is going to need to be in a place where she can lie down rather than being in a van for hours. Also, there will be a doctor on board that will monitor her and Amy while they're coming

here." He thanked Storm. *"No worries about that. I've also hired a nurse to go to Allen's home so that she'll get the best of care there as well. Also, I've made sure that the girls have their rooms set up. I cheated in looking into what they wanted, so it'll be something that they can have while getting rested up."*

"I can't thank you enough for this." She said that it had been her pleasure. She was looking forward to meeting Paige and her daughters. *"The girls are wonderful. Even though they've been through hell in the last few nights, they'll be having fun with Drew. He's been a good cousin to them."*

"Of course he is. He's a great kid." He thanked her again as he got dressed. The girls had all taken a shower before him, and he was happy that he'd remembered to get extra towels for all of them. They were headed to the hospital when Sable contacted him.

"You should see this house. It looks like a pink rocket exploded in the bedrooms." They laughed. *"I've gotten them some things like computers to use. I know that we might be doing too much, but I find that I don't care. I want them to have some fun while their mom is recovering."*

"They had so little when I picked them up. Everything

that the girls had was in a large trash bag. Their mother's wasn't much at all in that her things fit into a small box. I hurt for them." She said that she did too. *"All right, love. I'm going to see about feeding these little ones something bad for them and head over to the hospital. Hopefully, we'll be able to leave here sometime today. I hope so. I miss you."*

"I miss you too. I love you so much." He told her he loved her as well, and they closed the connection.

Paige was awake when they arrived, but he could almost taste her pain. She was refusing the meds in order to see her children. As soon as she was assured they were all fine, he insisted she takes something for it. She didn't argue with him but nodded. Calling in the nurse, Paige was drifting off almost as soon as the needle left the IV port.

Taking the kids to get some lunch, Garfield was enjoying himself. They were great kids, all four of them, and he was happy that they seemed to be bouncing back better than he was. Even Drew was able to have some fun with the girls.

It was three days later that they were able to leave the area. There had been a big shake-up at not only the police station but also the hospital. By the time they left, more than half of the administrative team had been fired, and all of the police department had been replaced with FBI agents that were called in to see into the allegations of theft, murder and a lot of other things he was just hearing about.

Once Paige and her daughters were settled into their new home, Garfield was finally able to feel better. He'd been so stressed out while down there that he'd never been so happy to be home in his life. Since he was so exhausted from it all, he and Sable laid down to nap. Snuggling up with her in their bed was the best thing that had happened all week. When he woke, not only was he alone, but there wasn't anyone in the house either. Getting up, he reached out to Sable to figure out where she had gone.

"I've been working on a project since you were gone. A hotline that abused people can call that will get them safely out of their situation. I didn't come up with the idea but this bunch of college men that put it out there that they'd be there for them if they called. Even going as far as moving them out of the place they were in to get them to a better place." He told her that was brilliant. *"I thought so too. Anyway, it's going to be a way that they can safely call into*

the hotline without the abuser knowing what is going on. I've not worked out the details on that as yet, but I'll get there."

"I have all the faith in the world that you will. I was thinking that this might be something my mom would like to help you with. She's been an advocate for helping the abused for a while now. You don't have to let her help you, but I'm sure she'd enjoy it." Sable told him that she was here with her now, helping with the details of it all. *"Great. Did you ask her about the baby? I'm sure she has lots of information for us."*

"Not only did she, but she said I should take your crib home with us the next time we're over. She said she has boxes of clothing that she's knitted over the years that she is going to divide up for all of the boys, she calls you guys." He said he thought that dad had made the beds for them all. *"He did. And the rocking chairs. When Charlie was making the first one for Edwin, he decided that he was going to make one for each of his children so that they could rock their own babies in when the time came. I think that's the sweetest thought ever. We'll be able to get it with the bed sometime."*

Garfield loved his parent so much, and the fact

that they had thought ahead by making it so that they would have a piece of their childhood when they had children made him think that they were the best parents ever. He hoped that he could be half the father that his dad had been, and he'd count himself lucky.

After having some early lunch, Garfield made his way to Allen's home. He was only there to make sure that they didn't need anything but hung around so that Allen could run to the store to get some much-needed supplies for his nieces.

"What sort of much-needed supplies do six year olds need?" Allen told him, then showed him the list they'd given him. "So they want to make their mom a card, and you need to get them...does this say fancy hearts? I'm not sure what that is, but you'd better not mess it up."

Amy, feeling much better, sat down next to him and explained. "We want the kind of hearts that look like paper cutouts. All fancy and stuff. I had one once, but it got blood on it when I lost a tooth. Oh, and we'd like some of those scissors that cut wavy lines and stuff too." She was adding to the list even as Allen was gathering up his wallet and car keys. "He's going to mess this up, huh?"

"Maybe, but you'll cut him some slack, right? I mean, it's been a long time since he's been around such beautiful little girls." She rolled her eyes at him. When Libby joined them at the table, she sat on his lap rather than taking the chair. He asked her if she thought he was a chair.

"No, but you don't hurt me when I'm close to you. I like that." He told her how sorry he was that she'd been treated like she'd been. "I'm not happy it happened, but we'll all still be together. That's what mom says all the time when the landlord would come over. Also, she said that what doesn't kill us makes us stronger. I think that's a bunch of bull crapola. Mom was beaten up all the time, and it didn't make her any stronger to fight back. Men are pigs."

"Not all of them are, honey. I'm not. Nor are my brothers." She eyed him, asking him how many brothers he had. "Five. All of us are big men, but we'd never hurt a woman. They're excited to get to meet you guys too."

"You should tell them to bring over some food, and we can have a cookout. We've never had one before." He asked her why not before he thought about it. "The landlord wouldn't allow us to have anything out on a grill. Mom tried to cook them in the stove once. The top of the oven got really red hot. But the stove broke, and we only had half-cooked hot dogs. Have you ever had macaroni salad? I've not."

The three of them were talking about all the things that went with a picnic when Glory came to join them. Of the three of them, Glory was the most shy. But when she had something to say, she wouldn't hesitate.

"I love chips. The kind that has sour cream on them. I had them once when I was really little, and I have been craving them since." He didn't know how little she could have possibly been at six, but he told her that was his mom's favorite too. "You don't like them?"

"I'm not a huge fan of chips at all, really. I know that my wife doesn't care for them either. Now French fries? I could eat a vat of them." They giggled and began talking about going to school soon and what they would do when it snowed. "We'll have to get you some winter stuff so we can go sledding. Mom and dad have a long hill behind their house that is the most fun of winter when it's covered in snow."

By the time Allen returned, he'd bet he knew more about the girls than their mother did. He knew what they liked and didn't like in the way of foods. The kind of clothing they preferred when it was hot out. He told them that he and Sable had a large pool they could use, and that excited them to no end.

He also found out more about their living conditions. The fact that their father didn't pay child support because he didn't believe they were his daughters. Garfield also understood something else about the three of them. They would scream at each other when they had a point to be made, but they'd kill someone if they tried to hurt one of the others. He thought that was the same as he and his brothers.

Allen returned with six large shopping bags of supplies. When he said he had more in the car, the girls followed him out. Garfield started emptying bags on the dining room table and separating out the items. Allen had found the fancy hearts, it seemed, and he got them in different sizes and colors. There were wavy scissors, lots of glitter, as well as glue and pipe cleaners. Garfield headed home before they started spreading the glitter around. There was no way he was going to be a sparkly wolf if he could help it. He knew that he'd never hear the end of it.

His heart was lighter as he headed home. He was also in a better mood. If he thought he could bottle up the girls' laughter and happiness, he'd never have to work another day in his life. It was like a good wine to him, to hear the laughter with no thought to how loud or crazy you sounded.

Before You Go...

HELP AN AUTHOR

write a review

THANK YOU!

Share your voice and help guide other readers to these wonderful books. Even if it's only a line or two, your reviews help readers discover the author's books so they can continue creating stories that you'll love. Log in to your favorite retailer and leave a review. Thank you.

AWARD WINNING, BESTSELLING AUTHOR

Kathi Barton, a winner of the Pinnacle Book Achievement Award and a best-selling author on Amazon and All Romance books, lives in Nashport, Ohio, with her husband, Paul. When not creating new worlds and romance, Kathi and her husband enjoy camping and going to auctions. She can also be seen at county fairs with her husband, an artist and potter.

Her muse, a cross between Jimmy Stewart and Hugh Jackman, brings her stories to life for her readers in a way that has them coming back time and again for more. Her favorite genre is paranormal romance, with a great deal of spice. You can visit Kathi online and drop her an email if you'd like. She loves hearing from her fans. aaronskiss@gmail.com.

Follow Kathi on her blog: http://kathisbartonauthor.blogspot.com/

www.ingramcontent.com/pod-product-compliance
Lightning Source LLC
Chambersburg PA
CBHW030222180626
46810CB00008B/2932